"Those pills ... **in my mind** ... **feeling the ja** ... **helps remind** ...

Nick's gaze lingered on Abby's mouth and his voice dropped low. "Reminds me that being here like this, with you and your family, isn't a damn dream, that I won't wake up to find myself strapped in some strange hospital bed."

Shaken, Abby stared at him. What horrors he must have gone through. The unguarded emotion in his gaze called to her on a completely different level. Unable to help herself, she rose on her tiptoes and pressed her lips against his. At first he seemed startled by her kiss, then, in an instant, he yanked her close and delved deep, as if he were a dying man and had been given his last sip of water.

Laura Iding loved reading as a child, and when she ran out of books she readily made up her own, completing a little detective mini-series when she was twelve. But, despite her aspirations for being an author, her parents insisted she look into a 'real' career, so the summer after she turned thirteen she volunteered as a Candy Striper and fell in love with nursing. Now, after twenty years of experience in trauma/critical care, she's thrilled to combine her career and her hobby into one—writing Medical Romances™ for Mills & Boon®. Laura lives in the northern part of the United States and spends all her spare time with her two teenage kids (help!), a daughter and a son, and her husband. Enjoy!

Recent titles by the same author:

A PERFECT FATHER
THE FLIGHT DOCTOR'S EMERGENCY*
THE FLIGHT DOCTOR'S LIFELINE*
THE FLIGHT DOCTOR'S RESCUE*

*Air Rescue

THE CONSULTANT'S HOMECOMING

BY
LAURA IDING

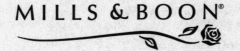

In loving memory of my mother, Janet Wanke,
who shared her love of reading with me.

First published in Great Britain 2006
Harlequin Mills & Boon Limited,
Eton House, 18-24 Paradise Road, Richmond, Surrey TW9 1SR

© Laura Iding 2006

Standard ISBN 0 263 84738 1
Promotional ISBN 0 263 85099 4

Set in Times Roman 10½ on 12¼ pt.
03-0406-44558

Printed and bound in Spain
by Litografia Rosés, S.A., Barcelona

PROLOGUE

March 14, 2005

AS SHE WALKED into her apartment, the phone rang. Abby Monroe frowned. Was someone from the hospital calling already? She'd just left. Had she forgotten to chart one of her meds? She dropped her bag and dashed across the room to pick up the receiver.

"Hello?"

"Abby?" Her older brother's voice sounded strange.

"Hi, Adam." She frowned. "Is something wrong?"

Silence. Alarm skittered across her nerves.

"Mom? Dad? Did something happen?"

"No, our parents are fine." His reassuring tone made her relax.

"What, then? I'm just walked in the door from work."

"It's Shane, Abby. He... There was a horrible accident—a plane crash in the mountains near Beijing and— Damn, Abby. He didn't make it."

No. Dear God, *no!*

Dazed, she sank to the floor. This couldn't be happening. There had to be some mistake. Shane was too young, only thirty-three, he couldn't possibly be dead. She shook her head, wanting to scream in protest, but Adam's heavy silence held her in check. She'd known Shane her entire life, mostly because Shane was her brother's best friend. For years, her parents treated Shane as if he were part of the family.

One day, she'd hoped to marry him, making Shane a part of the family for good.

"I'm sorry, Adam." She forced herself to ignore her own pain to consider what her brother was going through. "Are you all right?"

"Yeah. I guess." He didn't sound at all confident. "I still need to let Mom and Dad know."

"I'll be right over." No way was she letting Adam tell her parents alone.

"Thanks, Abby." Her brother sounded old. Tired.

She put down the phone then buried her face in her hands, allowing the keening sorrow and tears to come.

Her relationship with Shane had only just grown beyond friendship stage, but now he was gone.

For ever.

CHAPTER ONE

Four months later...

"COME ON, Mr Goetz, you're almost there," Abby encouraged the older man, who leaned heavily on his walker as he made his way slowly, painfully, down the hall toward the community dining room at the Veterans' Hospital's rehabilitation center.

"Bah, I ain't almost there." The stodgy old man scowled and set his walker down on the linoleum floor then shuffled his feet to catch up. "I don't know why you people don't let me eat in my room."

Abby couldn't help but smile. "Because we care too much about you to let you wallow in misery alone, that's why. Look at the bright sunlight pouring through the windows. It's a beautiful day."

One rubber corner of his walker stuck to the floor and he lost his balance, leaning heavily to his left side, his weak side.

"It's all right. I have you." Abby quickly tightened the muscles of her arm beneath his, supporting his weight the best she could while hanging onto the walker to keep it from toppling over. After a few tense minutes, Mr Goetz managed to get his left leg steadied beneath him and slowly shifted his weight so it was equally distributed.

Still, Abby didn't loosen her grip on his arm or the walker. "Are you all right, Mr Goetz? I promise, I won't let go until you are."

"Yeah, yeah. I got it." The near collision with the floor eased some of his crustiness. "I can make it."

"I know you can," she assured him. "And I'll be right here with you, the entire way."

The tomato scent of lasagne filled the air as they drew closer to the dining room. Another two steps and he managed to get into position to sit down at the table where three other men waited. Without any help, he eased into his seat.

"You did great, Mr Goetz." Abby moved his walker so it was out of the way, but not out of his reach. "I'm proud of you."

"You would be." Despite his earlier protests, his scowl eased into a smile and already he was in better spirits now that he was surrounded by his cronies. "When are you gonna marry me, Abby Monroe?"

She laughed. His proposal was as regular as the noontime meal. "Mr Goetz, you know my answer. I can't marry you, or anyone," she added, sternly eyeing the other men seated at the table, who often joined in, "until I've met my goal of traveling to all fifty states."

"Eh? What's so great about wanting to leave here?"

Mr Sutherland asked. "We all signed the petition so you would stay."

Abby barely refrained from rolling her eyes. "I'm not leaving for another five weeks, Mr Sutherland, so relax. Chances are, you'll be home long before then. And, please, stop signing petitions. This is my choice, not the Veterans' Hospital's decision."

"Abby?" One of the nurses gestured from the main desk. "Dr Roland is on the phone."

"Don't let him hang up. I'll be right there." Abby had paged the physical medicine specialist four times since the start of her shift to discuss Mr Goetz's care. She forced a smile on her face. "Enjoy your meal, gentlemen. And, remember, behave."

"Aw, Abby, what fun is that?" Mr Baker asked in a plaintive tone.

She laughed and shook her head as she left the dining room. Reaching over the desk, she pushed the blinking light on the multi-button phone. "Dr Roland? I've been calling you all morning."

"I'm busy."

She should have known he wouldn't apologize, and she bit her tongue, forcing herself to concentrate on the matter at hand. "The results of the urine sample we sent yesterday on Harold Goetz indicate he has another severe bladder infection. He needs another seven to ten day course of antibiotics. For some reason, we can't clear up this infection."

"Give him ten days of double-strength Bactrim. Is that all?" His dismissive tone infuriated Abby.

"I don't know. Are you going to bother calling back the next time I page you?" Abby challenged.

There was a moment of silence, then Dr Roland erupted. "Don't tell me how to run my unit. I always return my pages in good time and don't you dare insinuate otherwise." He slammed the phone in her ear.

"Ouch." Abby winced and hung up. "Boy, apparently the truth hurts."

Irene, the other nurse on the unit, stared at her with wide eyes. "I can't believe you said that to him."

"Yeah, well, I'm tired of him not answering my pages." Abby reached for Mr Goetz's chart so she could write the order. "If Roland ever made rounds, he'd know these things for himself, wouldn't he?" Irene nodded in agreement so Abby continued, "He hasn't shown his face around here for four days, at least not on day shift and not any other time either, according to the notes on the charts."

"I know. But still. I can't believe you actually said that to him." Irene was a newer graduate nurse, just three years younger than Abby, but at times like this Abby felt as if she were a hundred years older. "What if he complains to the boss about you?"

"Let him." Abby shrugged even though she knew Roland could cause trouble for her if he wanted to. Despite being absent more often than not, Dr Roland was still the medical director of the physical medicine rehab unit. Dealing with Roland was one of those things she wouldn't miss when she left to take her traveling nurse position in Florida. Although she was worried about what would happen to the patients when she was gone. If she didn't blow the whistle on Dr Roland, who would?

"Here, send this order down to the pharmacy." Abby handed the slip of paper to Irene. "And keep an eye on our patients. I'd better go see Leanne and let her know my side of the story, before Roland gets to her."

Irene gave a heavy sigh. "All right, but if she asks me, I'm going to have to tell her the truth about what I overheard you say."

"Don't worry, I won't ask you to lie for me," Abby reassured Irene. "I'll tell her exactly what I said myself, along with the fact he hasn't made rounds in days."

Abby flashed a grim smile. Considering she'd already given her notice and her last day of employment was August 15th, she didn't really care if her boss fired her, although if she did, the long-term patients would have a reason for their silly petition. Technically, she had nearly enough vacation time to cover the gap.

Go ahead, she thought, finding the nursing director's door and pounding on it, *make my day.*

Three hours later, the end of her shift came all too quickly. There were never enough hours in the day to get the work finished. Leanne had made her sign up for a counseling session about being more tactful when talking to the physicians. At least Leanne Walters hadn't yelled at her too much, plus she had promised to follow up with the chief of staff about Dr Roland's lack of rounds. As she headed home, Abby debated whether or not the chat would do any good. Surely she couldn't be the first nurse to complain about the guy.

Yet he was still there, getting paid for taking care of

his patients from the comfort of his easy chair on the other end of a phone rather than in person, using an actual stethoscope to do his own assessments.

The summer day was warm but not too hot as she walked the short six blocks home to her parents' house. She rolled her shoulders in an effort to ease the nagging ache. Grabbing Mr Goetz so he didn't fall had strained the muscles in her upper back. Again.

But she didn't dare think of complaining, not when she had to go home and help lift her incapacitated mother in and out of the bathtub. She stifled a sigh, immediately ashamed at the selfish thought.

Shane's death had taken a toll on their whole family. Abby had grieved for what would never be, then decided this was the perfect time to break loose from her family. To experience her dream of seeing the world. She'd always wanted to travel, but losing Shane had been hard. Then, just when things had begun to return to normal, her mother had tripped over their dog, Murphy, and fallen down the stairs.

Her mom's broken hip was healing slowly but surely. Her dad watched over her mother while Abby was at work, but he couldn't do everything himself. At least the fracture was on the mend. Soon her mother wouldn't need help at all.

Her parents had been upset by her decision to leave home and travel, but she couldn't let her love for them sway her from her goal. She'd lived vicariously through her older siblings for years, now it was time for her to do something for herself. She missed having her own apartment, having felt forced to give up her lease after her mother had broken her hip. There were also five other Monroe siblings to keep an eye on her parents.

Once she'd planned to travel with Shane. Her heart squeezed painfully in her chest. She'd known him her whole life, and just before he'd left for China, he'd kissed her, finally giving her a hint he was ready to take their relationship to the next level. Waiting for Shane to return home had been pure agony. Still, she hadn't blamed him for jumping at the chance to participate in a special surgical training program in Beijing.

Losing him felt surreal. Any minute, she expected him to vault onto the porch of her parents' house, demanding to know what was for dinner.

A heavy ache settled in her heart. She missed him.

As she approached her parents' house, she noticed a man with a cane, who looked to be in his early thirties, standing and staring at the house number on a plaque at the edge of the road. He was tall, at least six feet, his back ramrod straight and his dark hair cut military short. For a moment she wondered if he was a lost soldier looking for the Veterans' Hospital, then realized his worn jeans and T-shirt wasn't anything close to a uniform.

He didn't seem to notice her until she was right next to him. With a polite smile, she greeted him. "Hello, may I help you? Are you lost?"

"Uh, yes. I'm looking for the Monroe house, and for Abigail Monroe."

Her eyes widened. "I'm Abby Monroe."

"Oh." He frowned, trailing his gaze over her. "I expected someone...older."

She bit back a flash of impatience. She was twenty-six, not sixteen, and more than a little tired of people assuming the latter. "Well, I'm not expecting anyone," she countered. "What can I do for you?"

Belatedly, she noticed a dark blue duffel bag on the ground at his feet. He leaned down and carefully extracted a battered cigar box. His facial expression didn't change as he straightened, but she sensed he was in excruciating pain the way each movement was slow and deliberate. With a solemn expression, he held out the box to her. "I have something that belongs to you. I'm sorry it took me so long to bring this, I was…unwillingly detained."

She didn't know who this guy was, and she was too tired to care. Crossing her arms over her chest, she silently refused his dubious offering. "Who are you? Why would you have anything that belongs to me?"

"I'm Nick Tremayne, a friend of Shane Reinhart's. This box contains letters and e-mail messages you sent to Shane during the time we were both on a six-month surgical training stint in Beijing." A tick spasmed in his cheek and his tone revealed no emotion as he added, "I'm very sorry for your loss."

Nick hoped she'd take the damn box before he made a fool of himself by falling flat on his face. Every muscle in his leg screamed in agony. The bright sunlight beating down on his bare head echoed the throbbing in his thigh and sweat beaded on his upper lip.

Shane's girlfriend finally took the cigar box from his hands. His arm dropped to his side and he nearly closed his eyes in relief. He'd overtaxed his injured muscles by

traveling halfway across the country without the help of
his pain meds.

"Are you OK?" The girl, who had looked all of
sixteen with her strawberry blond hair pulled into a
ponytail and the sprinkling of freckles across her nose,
leaned toward him, a frown marring her pretty brow.
"You'd better sit down."

He must be losing his touch. He could have sworn
he hadn't revealed any sign of his pain. Nick forced
himself to look into the girl's concerned blue eyes. "I
don't need to sit down."

"Look, Mr Tremayne, I'm a nurse and I know for a
fact you need to sit before you fall." She gestured to the
steps of a wide porch in front of an old white farmhouse.
"There's some shade from the sun over here."

Damned if he didn't find himself turning and walking
stiffly toward the proffered shade. "Dr Tremayne."

"Excuse me?" She set the cigar box beside her as she
settled on the top step. A large Irish setter came
bounding out the door, wagging his tail in greeting.

Idly, he reached out to pet the friendly dog, before
bending awkwardly to take a seat on the steps beside
her. "Never mind, call me Nick." Taking the weight off
his leg brought immeasurable relief and, despite his
goal of not letting on how much he hurt, he used his
good hand to massage the tense muscles.

"Nick. Of course." He almost smiled when she
tapped herself on the forehead with the palm of her
hand. "I remember now. Shane mentioned you in several
of his letters. You're a trauma surgeon too, aren't you?"

All thoughts of smiling faded. Damn. He had to

remember why he was here. To pay his respects to Shane's girlfriend. Mentally bracing himself, he turned so he could face her. "I was."

"But not any more?"

He swallowed hard and shook his head. "Not exactly." Without thinking, he opened and closed his injured hand into a fist. His arm was coming along much better than his leg, but he was so far from being well, he couldn't imagine setting foot in an operating room. "At the moment, I'm more of a patient than a doctor."

"Hmm." Despite the strawberry blond hair and freckles, he suspected those intense blue eyes of hers didn't miss a thing. "And you came all the way to Milwaukee, Wisconsin, to give me a cigar box filled with letters and messages I sent to Shane?"

"Yes" He had a strong desire to tell her the rest, to explain everything, but the words stuck in his throat. The truth was his burden to bear—nothing good would come of telling Shane's girlfriend what he knew.

Shane Reinhart's death had been his fault.

CHAPTER TWO

A LITTLE girl with blond pigtails ran out of the house, banging the screen door behind her. "Aunt Abby, Grandma wants to know what's taking you so long." Her eyes rounded in shocked surprise when she saw Nick sitting there. "Aunt Abby! Don'cha know, you're not supposed to talk to strangers?"

"Yes, Beth. But Dr Tremayne isn't a stranger, he's a friend." Nick almost smiled at how Abby stretched the truth for the child's benefit. "Tell Grandma I'll be in soon." The girl dashed inside, and with an apologetic glance at Nick, Abby added, "Mom broke her hip a month ago and she needs help getting around."

He understood she'd just given him his cue to leave. "Shane mentioned how the Monroe family was closer to him than his own. I can certainly see why he felt that way. Please, give your parents my regards."

"Why don't you stay for dinner?" Abby stood with a fluid movement he sorely envied. "My brother Adam is coming over—he was a good friend of Shane's. I'm sure he'd love to talk to you."

Sucking in a deep breath to ward off the anticipated pain, Nick pushed himself to a standing position. A dark red-hot jolt of pain flashed before his eyes, momentarily blinded him. Damn, something as easy as standing shouldn't be so difficult. To distract himself from his weakness, he focused his gaze on Abby's youthful face as he recited her brothers' names. "Aaron, Adam, Alec, Austin and Abby. Don't tell me, let me guess. You guys are the A-team."

Abby laughed, and the simple motion lit up her whole face, making him suck in another quick breath. "What can I say? My parents have a strange sense of humor. You forgot my sister, Alaina. Beth is her daughter, she's between Aaron and Adam. I have the dubious privilege of being the youngest. My sister has carried on the tradition, her children are Bethany and Benjamin. We can only pray she doesn't have four more. I'm not sure our family gatherings could take the noise."

He thought her family sounded wonderful. He'd heard bits and pieces about the Monroe family from Shane. Guilt over his death returned in full force. "You're lucky to have such a large family," he told her sincerely.

For a moment, her expression softened. "Yeah, I know."

"Abby?" A booming male voice came from inside the house. "Beth tells me your boyfriend is here. Why don't you invite him in?" As he spoke, her father opened the door and stepped out on the porch. "You know your friends are always welcome. My name is Abe Monroe." Her dad held out his hand. "Pleased to meet you."

"Nick Tremayne, and it's nice to meet you, too."

Nick shook Abby's father's hand, subtly shifting his weight to ease the pain in his left leg before it buckled and he embarrassed himself by doing an ungainly somersault off the side of the porch.

"He's actually a friend of Shane's." Abby rolled her eyes at her dad's assumption. "He's a surgeon too and was training with Shane over in Beijing. I just invited him to stay for dinner," she added while opening the door. "Dad, talk him into it while I run up to see Mom."

"Really?" The older man's eyes brightened with keen interest as he looked at Nick. Abby grinned slyly as she left him alone with her father. "You were with Shane in Beijing? I'd love to hear about your time there, if you don't mind."

Nick would swear he heard the clang of a jail door slamming shut behind him. How was he going to get out of this? For a moment, he considered simply walking away, then realized he owed the Monroes more than a couple of minutes of his time. Shane had called them his surrogate family. So what if he didn't have his pain meds and muscle relaxants with him? They didn't work all that well anyway. He could suffer for a few more hours.

He didn't have anywhere else to go. Except back to an empty motel room. For years he'd roamed the world, thriving on his independence. But since his accident he'd become keenly aware of his lack of a home. A family.

"No, sir, I don't mind at all." He forced a smile. "I'd love to stay for dinner."

"Great! Come on in, then." Abe gave a hearty laugh and opened the door, gesturing for Nick to come in. "I'll tell Alaina to set another place at the table."

Nick followed Abby's father inside the house and immediately felt surrounded by the warmth of the Monroe family. One entire wall of the living room was covered with framed pictures of the children, including, he saw with a grimace, several pictures of Shane.

And, of course, dozens of Abby.

In his opinion, she was by far the cutest of the bunch.

He felt like a horrible traitor stepping into this wholesome homestead. When he heard the distinct sound of Abby's laughter, he knew he was sunk.

His mission of returning the cigar box to Abby had been completed. He had no intention of telling the family the graphic details about the plane crash that had nearly killed him and had eventually stolen Shane's life. The hotel had sent his bags on to the hospital in the US but had mixed up some of his and Shane's belongings. He wasn't even sure how it happened, some phrase caught his eye and he'd ended up reading part of a letter. Then he'd suffered complications from surgery that had extended his stay in the hospital for another two months. Abby's letters were what kept him from losing his mind during the long, painful weeks of rehab. He'd read each letter so often he could quote them by memory.

Bad enough he'd betrayed her privacy. What was he doing hanging around here?

Meeting Abby in person hadn't helped exorcise his demons. In fact, just the opposite. Now that he'd met her in person, he only wanted to stay.

Abby couldn't concentrate on taking care of her mother, not when she could hear the rumble of Nick's deep voice downstairs as he spoke to her family. She was more than a little intrigued by the tall, dark-haired stranger.

Although he really wasn't a stranger, she corrected. That hadn't been just a line to satisfy her niece. Shane had mentioned Nick several times in his letters, how they'd go out and play tourist in Beijing after putting in long, grueling hours in the operating room. Shane had also been impressed by Nick's skill as a surgeon. Such a shame he'd been injured.

"Ouch!" her mother yelped.

"Oh, I'm so sorry." Abby winced and pulled her attention back to the task of getting her mother out of the bathtub. "I didn't mean to knock your knee like that. Here, wrap your arm around my shoulder so I can support your weight off your hip."

"That's all right, dear." Abby's mother gave her a forgiving smile. "Did you have a rough day at work?"

"No more than usual." More careful now, Abby helped her mother stand, then get out of the bathtub. According to the physical therapists, they weren't supposed to rely on the automatic lift any more, even though her mother preferred the ease of using the supportive equipment.

"I'm falling," she cried, waving her arm when she lost her balance.

"Don't worry, I have you," Abby soothed. She tightened her grip on her mother's tiny frame. Thank heavens, her mother was small-boned. "You're doing great, Mom. A few more weeks and you'll be getting in and out of the tub on your own."

"I'm not so sure about that." Her mom sat heavily in the chair with a sigh. "Maybe you should put off leaving for another couple of months. You know, Alaina could use your help with the kids once in a while, with her husband away."

Abby bit back the automatic protest. She knew her mother wasn't trying to make her feel guilty.

But the end result was a pretty impressive guilt trip, just the same.

"Here, let's get you dressed. We have a guest for dinner."

"Really?" Her mother perked up, diverted by the prospect of company, as Abby had hoped. "Who?"

"Dr Nick Tremayne. He's a friend of Shane's." Abby wrapped her mother in a robe. "Let's get you into the bedroom and you can tell me what you'd like to wear."

"A friend of Shane's?" her mother echoed, using the walker to make her way from the bathroom into the bedroom. "Oh, my."

Oh, my, was right. Her impression exactly, Abby thought with a wry grin. Men hadn't been high on her list of priorities after Shane's death, but she wouldn't be female if she hadn't noticed Nick Tremayne.

Not that she was interested in anything except hearing about his travels. Her pulse quickened at the thought. Beijing! How she'd longed to see the Forbidden City and the Ming tombs Shane had described in his letters. She could just imagine what it must have been like to travel through a country where you couldn't even speak the language. For too long now, she'd lived vicariously through others.

Soon she'd start her traveling nurse assignment.

She'd be happy to at least see the breadth of the United States, but she'd already begun to save money to travel overseas as well.

Her feet itched to shake the Wisconsin dust off the bottom of her soles once and for all. Not that she wouldn't return home for visits but, as the youngest, she'd been forced to wait as one by one her siblings and, of course, Shane, had taken off for adventures unknown.

Alaina had come back once she'd decided to marry Scott, and still Abby hadn't managed to find her way across state lines. First she'd needed enough nursing experience behind her to qualify for a traveling nurse assignment. Then Shane's death, followed by her mother's broken hip, had postponed her plans. Of course, if her family had their way, she'd never leave. They'd keep trying to run her life, refusing to believe she was capable of surviving on her own.

As far as she was concerned, she'd be just fine without them. She longed to get away. She could practically taste the spicy southern cuisine, feel the salty spray on her face as she stood on the rocky shores of the Atlantic Ocean.

Her heart raced with anticipation. She could hardly wait.

Abby listened in awe as Nick described his and Shane's trip to the Great Wall of China. She imagined how the winding wall must have looked, zig-zagging like a snake through the green, hilly mountain. Suddenly, moving to Florida sounded far too tame.

Maybe she needed to reconsider her initial goal of

seeing all fifty states. There would always be plenty of time to travel her homeland, but going overseas now, while she was young enough to explore the sites, was sounding better and better. Were traveling nurse assignments available overseas? How different could the nurse's responsibilities be? She thought about some of the European medical articles she'd read. Pretty different. So much for that idea.

"Thanks for dinner," Nick was saying now. "I very much enjoyed the home-cooked meal." Alaina preened at his praise. "But I really need to get going."

Abby could tell her father was disappointed, but he gave in gracefully. "Of course you do. Ah...how long will you be in town?"

"I'm not sure, probably only a few days." Nick flashed him an apologetic smile. "If I have time, I'll stop back before I leave."

"If you do, Dad will just ply you with more questions about what it's like to live in Beijing," Adam warned.

"A short visit would be fine." Her father seemed mollified by Nick's half-hearted promise.

"Did you park your car nearby?" Abby asked, recalling how she'd found him standing outside their home. She didn't remember seeing any strange cars parked in the road, but she could have missed it. "I'll walk you outside."

Adam raised a brow. "I'll come with you."

Oh, please. Like she needed a chaperon for this? "I can handle it." Her narrow glare told him to back off. Her brothers and their protective attitude had worn thin years ago. They always seemed to find fault with the guys she dated, except for Shane, and while Shane had kissed her, he hadn't actually ever asked her out. Although not for lack of trying on her part.

Her brothers routinely interfered with other aspects of her life as well. Even when she'd gotten her own apartment, Alec, now a cop, had moved into the same building to keep an eye on her, claiming the area had a high crime rate. Right. She really needed to gain some independence from her family. Being forced to temporarily move in with her parents wasn't helping at all.

"Actually, I didn't drive here." Nick's smile seemed strained. "The motel I'm staying at isn't far."

Normally, she would have agreed. It was a nice summer's night for a walk after all. But she'd noticed the lines bracketing Nick's mouth had grooved deeper as dinner had worn on. She worked with enough patients experiencing pain that she recognized a man in agony when she saw him. She wondered if he'd brought any medications with him, or if he'd left them at the motel.

He stood and swayed slightly before using one hand to force his knee into a locked position beneath him. Yep. Definitely left them at the hotel, she decided. Stupid, stubborn man, not to have said anything sooner.

"I'll walk you out," she repeated, ignoring her brothers. For a moment she thought Adam was going to follow, but he didn't. Thank heavens Alec was working or for sure he would have. Alec saw violent crime everywhere he looked, making him twice as cautious at home. As she strode past the door, she lifted her parents' car keys off the hook mounted on the wall.

She'd sold her car, intent on buying another one when she'd settled in Florida, if she needed one. Actually, since the condo she would staying in was located close to the hospital, she wasn't sure she did. Maybe she'd buy a bike instead. Or an electric scooter. Something she could use to ride down to the beach....

Outside, Nick crossed the porch, then descended the stairs, one painful step at a time.

"Hop in and I'll drive you to the hotel," she told him, gesturing to the vehicle parked in the driveway.

"I can walk. Thanks again for dinner." Nick's tone was abrupt, almost rude.

If she hadn't been so used to taking care of people in pain, she might have taken his dismissal personally. Luckily, in dealing with her patients and the Dr Rolands of the world, she'd grown tough.

"Don't be a fool. Get in the car," she spoke sharply. "For Pete's sake, do you think I can't see how badly you're hurting?"

Nick paused, then turned to look at her, as if he couldn't believe her gall. Then understanding dawned. "That's right. I almost forgot, you're a nurse."

Her smile was not a bit sweet. "Yes, and if you know what's good for you, you won't argue. Especially not when you look as if one little push would send you sprawling flat on your face."

His jaw tightened and she knew he hated every minute of weakness. But, hallelujah, he didn't bite her head off, turning instead to hobble toward the car. "Fine, you can drive me back."

She didn't smirk, but simply waited until he'd slid into the passenger seat, before climbing in on the driver's side. She adjusted the seat and backed out of the driveway.

"So, where are you staying?" she asked, ignoring the resentment radiating off him in waves.

"The Cozy Inn. It's just six blocks east and one block south of here."

"The Cozy Inn?" She glanced at him in surprise. "That's right across the street from the Veterans' Hospital where I work."

His gaze was enigmatic. "I know."

She was dying of curiosity. "So what are you doing here in Milwaukee? Other than returning way letters, that is."

"Nothing much." He stared out the window, as if avoiding her gaze. "I told you, I'm not practicing as a surgeon at the moment. I'm still in physical therapy."

"I see." But she really didn't. Drumming her fingers on the steering wheel, she sent him a sidelong glance. Had he come to Milwaukee for a second opinion maybe? She wanted to ask, but that would be rude.

Wouldn't it? Yes. Definitely rude.

"Here we are, The Cozy Inn." She pulled into the hotel parking lot. "Where's your room?"

"Ground level, number six." The hotel was small, only two rows of rooms behind a glass-enclosed hallway. In deference to his discomfort, Abby pulled into the parking slot closest to the doorway of room six.

She watched as Nick opened the door and tried to swing his legs out of the car. As he struggled, he never uttered a sound, but she noticed his forehead was covered with a fine sheen of sweat.

Ridiculous, the guy would fall on this backside before requesting a hand. With a muttered oath Abby shot out of the car and swung around to the passenger side.

"I can't stand it." She sighed and glared at him. "It's your left side that's giving you problems, right?"

Remaining mute, lips compressed in a tight line, he nodded.

"That's what I thought. I'll pull you up, then I want you to lean on me." She used both of her hands to clasp his right hand and used her weight to lever him off the seat.

He was several shades paler by the time he managed to stand upright. She braced her body under his good arm, so she didn't stress the injured muscles of his left side. Keeping her pace slow, they walked toward the doorway.

He was heavier than he looked, probably because of his height. She wasn't sure how they managed to get the glass door open, but soon they were inside, standing in front of his hotel room door. He had his room key and was fitting it into the lock with his left hand, trying hard not to sway. She imagined anyone walking past them would think Nick had had too much to drink.

"All right, we're almost there," she encouraged as he finally pushed the door open.

Inside, she was glad the room was on the small side as they made their way toward the bed. She was beginning to feel his weight, her own sore muscles protesting the strain.

"Here, let's turn so you can sit down." She tried to help him pivot, but somehow her legs twined with his and she felt him tilt sideways.

"No," she cried as she attempted to yank him upright, but too late. His heavier weight dragged her down along with him as they bounced on the bed in a helpless tangle of limbs.

CHAPTER THREE

ONCE the blinding pain receded, Nick wondered if he'd died and gone to heaven. Not because the pain had lessened to a tolerable level but because of Abby's warm vanilla scent filling his head and the softness of her breasts pressed against his chest. She was sprawled on top of him, her light weight more than welcome. He prayed she wouldn't move. Her pert mouth invited him close.

He didn't know what possessed him to lift up the necessary inch to taste her. But once he did, he couldn't make himself regret it. She was sweet, her lips soft and moist. When she didn't pull away or slug him, he gathered her close and took advantage of her startled gasp to deepen the kiss.

How long since he'd held a woman? Or even wanted to? It seemed like a lifetime.

Her eager response as she kissed him back sent his blood thundering to his head and to the area below his belt. Warning signals bleeped in his brain and all too soon he realized he'd started something he didn't dare finish.

Abby wasn't his woman to have. She belonged to

someone else. Before he could talk himself out of it, he broke off the kiss. Dazed, she stared down at him for a long moment, before she rolled off him to sit on the edge of the bed. She looked stunned, shaken.

Damn. He shouldn't have taken advantage of her like that. He'd been only thinking of himself. Again.

With a wince, he sat up next to her. As she still hadn't said a word, he felt obligated to apologize. "I'm sorry. I never should have kissed you, especially when you're grieving over losing Shane. I know it's too soon. Just chalk this up to a moment of insanity."

Her entire body went still. Then he realized his mistake. Stupid, stupid, stupid! The only reason he knew the extent of her feelings toward Shane was because he'd read her letters.

I miss you, Shane. Things aren't the same around here without you. I especially miss our talks. Have I mentioned what a great listener you are? Even now, writing to you like this isn't the same as the two of us laughing and talking for hours. Especially the night right before you left.

He'd become envious of the relationship between Abby and Shane. That's how low he'd sunk, battling a burning resentment toward a dead man.

"What do you know about my feelings for Shane?" Abby's voice held a deceptive softness, but the glitter in her blue eyes betrayed her true feelings.

He swallowed hard. "Ah…I just figured. I mean, Shane told me how romantically involved the two of you were…"

"Nice try, but I don't believe Shane said anything of the sort." Confusion flickered across her features, then her gaze narrowed as realization dawned. "I don't believe it. You read my letters to Shane."

Here it was. He braced himself for the full force of her anger because he deserved it. "Yes. I didn't mean to, but I did. Read them, I mean. I'm sorry."

"Of all the low-life stunts." Face flaming, Abby scrambled to her feet and shot across the motel room to the door. "Those letters were *personal*. You had no right to read them."

"I know." Helpless to do anything else, he watched her storm out of his room, slamming the door behind her for good measure.

He wanted to run after her, to make her understand why he'd read them, but instead he let her go, feeling very much like the lowest form of life on earth. With a sigh, he scrubbed his hands over his face. He couldn't find the words to explain how her letters had changed him. Her positive outlook on life, her self-deprecating humor and her obvious affection for her family had gotten him through the darkest days of his recovery. Every letter had only endeared her to him more. Until he'd yearned to meet her in person.

Now that he had, she was even more beautiful than he'd imagined. Meeting her in the street outside the Monroe house, he'd experienced an instant attraction even though she'd looked far too young. He wanted her in a way he hadn't wanted any woman in a long time. The way their brief kiss had spun out of control only proved the point.

Too bad, he was now the last man on the face of the earth she would be interested in.

Even if she got over her anger and embarrassment of how he'd read her letters, there was still no use pursuing a relationship. For one thing, he was still a cripple, but, worse, Abby didn't know the truth.

If not for Shane's attempts to rescue him, Shane would still be alive today.

How dared Nick Tremayne read her person letters to Shane? What right did he have to invade her privacy?

What right did he have to kiss her?

Abby jammed her keys into the ignition, missing the keyhole not just once but three times.

Mortified, she leaned her forehead on the steering wheel and tried to get herself under control. First Nick's kiss had rocked her off balance. Then to find out he'd read her letters— She swallowed hard. So what if the letters were more on a friendship level? They were still personal. She and Shane hadn't been lovers, or this could have been far worse. A strangled laugh escaped from her throat. As if it wasn't bad enough.

Nick probably thought she was hopeless, the way she'd hinted at wanting a deeper relationship with Shane. She'd vented her frustrations over her dull life and her interfering, overprotective family. Good grief, no wonder Nick had expected someone older. A boring, bitter old maid.

Enough! No use wallowing in self-pity. With a determined motion she pulled herself together. She would forget about the impact of Nick's heated kiss and his blatant disregard for her privacy. Lifting her head, she slid the key into the ignition and started the car. Calmer now, she drove home. It was easy to admit that she was more embarrassed than angry to discover Nick knew all those unflattering things about her.

Not until she'd pulled into her parents' driveway, though, did the question really occur to her.

Why?

Why would Nick Tremayne, a trauma surgeon stationed in Beijing, bother to read letters she'd written to Shane Reinhart?

She stared past the rakes and shovels hanging off the back wall of the garage. She had no clue. To be honest, she couldn't think of one single, logical reason for Nick to care about what she'd written.

Perturbed, she climbed from the car and headed inside the house. Abby wasn't in the habit of lying to herself, so she forced herself to examine her true feelings. Was she more embarrassed over her response to Nick's kiss or the way he'd read her letters?

Both. And she couldn't quite pinpoint which of the two bothered her more.

"Mr Goetz, it's time for you to go down for physical therapy." Abby stopped the older man in the wheelchair from going in the opposite direction. "That's the way to the dining room. The elevators are down the hall, this way." She spun him back around.

"I'm not going to therapy." He glared at her, then with surprising strength spun himself so he was headed to the dining room again. "I'm too tired for therapy."

Abby suppressed a sigh. She understood how difficult it was for these patients to force themselves to face the pain of physical therapy, yet at the same time they'd never get any better if they didn't work the injured muscles. The image of Nick flashed in her mind's eye. He could have used a few hours of physical therapy, too, and she wondered again why he'd come to Milwaukee. Had he come to see a specialist? Or was he still under a doctor's care at home?

Where did Nick call home?

"Mr Goetz, you know the rules," Abby explained again. A big part of being accepted to the rehabilitation floor meant tolerating three hours of therapy per day. He might be one of her favorite patients, but this was for his own good. "You have to go to therapy, even if only for a short while. Unless you're sick in bed, which you obviously aren't."

For a moment the old man glared at her, then his shoulders slumped. "I'm just too tired, Abby."

Her heart squeezed in sympathy but she steeled her resolve. "I know. But you need to at least give it a try. Please? Once you're in the gym, working your muscles, I'm sure you'll feel less tired. And if not, tell the therapist to call me so I can run down and get you."

He let out a deep, heavy sigh. "All right." He allowed her to turn his chair around and wheel him down the hall toward the elevators. Abby had a million other things to do, but she wheeled Mr Goetz into the elevator and rode down with him.

When the doors opened, she pushed his chair down the hall and into the spacious gym area. Equipment of all kinds lined the walls, including some exercise machines. Wide exercise mats were scattered around the center of the room for muscle strengthening activities. A set of parallel bars for independent standing and walking stood on the opposite side of the room. For a second, a man with his back to her, using the bars, reminded her of Nick. Then she laughed at her own foolishness. She was imagining him everywhere. The guy haunted her because of one simple, silly kiss.

Paul, one of the physical therapists on duty, crossed the room and greeted his patient. "Good morning, Mr Goetz. How are you feeling today?"

She hadn't seen Paul since the last time he'd asked her out, but she forced a smile and gave her head a slight shake. "Mr Goetz isn't feeling very energetic today. Maybe you can start him off slow, hmm?"

Paul flashed her a questioning glance, but nodded. "Sure thing. We'll work on the floor mat first—how about that?"

"I guess so." Mr Goetz was less than enthused.

"Thanks," she told Paul, then reached down to gently squeeze Mr Goetz's arm. "Take care. I'll see you upstairs in a little while."

Paul wheeled Mr Goetz toward the mat and she stared after them for a minute. Paul was a nice guy, but she couldn't summon any interest in him, there was no spark of attraction at all. At the time, she'd wondered if she'd ever get over losing Shane.

Until she'd met Nick.

Her cheeks flushed as she remembered being in Nick's motel room. Apparently, she wasn't immune to a great-looking guy after all. Her body had betrayed her by responding to Nick's embrace. Good grief, the man could kiss. Never had her heart gone from zero to ninety like that, leaving her wanting more.

As much as it pained her to admit it, Shane's kiss hadn't roused such an instantaneous response.

Thank goodness, Nick had broken off the kiss before she'd been able to give in to the impulse of her desire. Her embarrassment could have been so much worse.

She swallowed hard and turned away. Just because her body had betrayed her, it didn't mean she was interested in anything personal with the guy. She couldn't wait to get out on her own, and a relationship would interfere with her traveling. Besides, Nick wasn't her type. She liked friendly, outgoing guys like Shane. Guys who liked to have long talks, who were comfortable to be around. Maybe Shane's kiss hadn't rocked her world, but he fit her personality far better. Tall, dark and brooding didn't appeal to her.

Too bad, because Nick was devastatingly attractive. From a purely physical perspective, of course.

Shaking off the useless thoughts, Abby decided to take the stairs up to the second-floor rehab unit. She'd gotten all the way to the top of the stairs and halfway down the hall toward the rehab unit when the overhead speaker came on.

"Code blue, first floor, physical therapy gym. Code blue, first floor, physical therapy gym."

"Mr Goetz!" Abby knew with a sixth sense that her patient was in trouble. Although she wasn't a part of the code blue team, she raced back down the stairs to the first floor.

She burst into the gym area and saw a group of

people crowded around a physical therapy floor mat. She pushed her way into the center. "What happened?"

"He's having a seizure." Nick glanced up at her from where he sat beside Mr Goetz. "Does he take medication for seizures?"

She was startled to find Nick there, dressed in light gray sweats, and realized her mind hadn't been playing tricks on her after all. She forced herself to think back over Mr Goetz's medical history. "No, he doesn't. He's never had a seizure before that I'm aware of."

"Good to know." Nick's attention was focused on the patient. "Where's the code cart? I want the intubation equipment ready once this seizure has passed."

"I have it right here." Paul opened the bottom drawer of the blue box cart next to him and pulled out a smaller bin holding some equipment and set it beside Nick.

"Maybe we should intubate him now?" Abby placed a hand on Mr Goetz's body, feeling each tremor down to the soles of her feet. "He's not breathing very well."

"I can't intubate him until after the seizure. His jaw muscles are locked tight."

She could sense Nick's frustration, and as they both stared at Mr Goetz, his face seemed to grow dusky. She found herself holding her own breath. Would his heart handle the strain?

"The code team should be here any minute," Paul informed them.

Abby knew the physical therapy gym was located on the opposite side of the building from the ICUs, where the respondents were coming from.

The movement beneath her hand stopped. She glanced up at Nick. "The seizure is over."

"I'm going to intubate him. He's already post-ictal." Nick reached for the equipment he'd already set up. "Abby, held hold him steady."

Did Nick have practice privileges here? Though breaking policy was a minor issue compared to the threat of losing Mr Goetz's life.

"What else can I do?" She didn't have critical-care experience, but understood the basics.

"Connect the heart monitor while I give him some breaths with the ambu-bag." Nick had already hooked up the ambu-bag to the portable oxygen tank on the code cart.

"All right." Her fingers fumbled with the unfamiliar task, but soon she had the electrodes placed. The beeping of Mr Goetz's heart once she'd turned on the monitor was reassuring.

Nick gave one last breath then set the ambu-bag aside and reached for the laryngoscope. Abby held onto Mr Goetz while Nick opened the elderly man's mouth and peered into the back of his throat to visualize the trachea. With a deft movement he slid the breathing tube down Mr Goetz's throat.

The beeping on the heart monitor slowed down.

Abby gasped. "I think his rhythm is changing."

The rest of the code team arrived.

"Do you need help?" the resident physician asked between panting breaths from his dash over from the ICU.

"Yeah, give him a milligram of atropine." Nick finished inserting the endotracheal tube, then pulled the stylet out. "Quick, Abby, hand me the Easycap so we can check the tube placement."

When placed on the end of the endotracheal tube, the device changed color if correctly placed in the patient's airway and not his stomach. Abby slid the device on the end of the tube, and sighed in relief when the yellow color confirmed the tube was in the correct place.

"The tube is good." She took the device off, then connected the ambu-bag to the endotracheal tube. "Listen for breath sounds, too."

"I need a stethoscope."

The resident who'd run to the code handed his over.

Nick listened as Abby gave big breaths with the ambu-bag. She watched the monitor. Mr Goetz's heartbeat gradually improved with the delivery of oxygen. "I hear breath sounds on both sides. Let's hold off on the atropine."

"He needs to be transferred to the ICU." The resident took over the situation. "What happened?"

Abby answered, "A seizure, although he doesn't have a history of seizures." A detail that continued to nag at her. What could possibly have caused him to have a seizure? "He's in rehab because of a total hip replacement. He was due to go to a nursing home in a week, but he's on a waiting list. His chart is right here. I can get the rest of his stuff out of his room and bring it up to the ICU."

"Sounds good." The transport team had responded with a gurney so once Mr Goetz's airway was secure, they transferred him from the gym mat to the cart.

Abby stood back, allowing the code team to take Mr

Goetz away. She glanced at Nick, who used his cane to help him stand. "I'm surprised to see you here, but thank heavens you were around to help."

He shrugged. "I'm still getting therapy three times a week. I've been employed by the government for years, which gives me certain privileges to be treated at any veterans' hospital."

"I see." So his choice of motel, directly across from the hospital, wasn't accidental. Hope flared. "Does that mean you have practice privileges here?"

He shrugged. "Technically, yeah. I'm on medical leave as far as being a surgeon goes, but I still have a license to practice medicine."

"Mr Goetz didn't want to go to therapy this morning." She voiced her deepest concern. "I made him come down, then heard the code blue being called."

Nick placed a comforting hand on her arm. "It's not your fault. If he had a seizure, there's a medical reason for it."

"I know." She thought back over Mr Goetz's rehab stay. "Now that you mention it, he complained of headaches a few times over the past week." Doubt swelled, stealing the breath from her lungs. Had she missed something important?

"Did the rehab doctors work up his headaches?" Nick asked.

"No, we just gave him Tylenol to treat them. Besides, Dr Roland doesn't make rounds very often."

Nick's gaze sharpened. "What do you mean?"

She bit her lip, hesitated, then shrugged. Heck, she'd started this, she may as well finish it. "Just what I said.

Dr Roland doesn't make rounds very often. In fact, if we didn't have to call him with issues, we wouldn't even know he was the physician of record."

CHAPTER FOUR

SWEAT rolled off Nick's forehead, burning his eyes as he worked his injured leg on the exercise equipment. He tried to wipe his brow on the short sleeve of his T-shirt without losing his grip. He hung onto the dual hand-grips, using everything he had in him to lever the weights up. The weights were only set at a measly twenty pounds but each repetition felt like some maso-chist had moved the pin to a hundred pounds.

The blazing pain radiating through his body re-minded him of the plane crash, when he'd spent count-less hours wedged in the plane wreck, struggling to crawl out despite his broken pelvis, multiple compound fractures of his left leg and left dislocated shoulder.

Working the sore muscles now, he knew he was lucky to be alive. A life he owed to Shane Reinhart. Most of the time he'd spent in the hospital was a dark blur. After his initial emergency surgery in China, he'd been trans-ferred back to the States, courtesy of the US govern-ment. There were times it paid to be employed by Uncle Sam. That's when he'd received his box of personal be-

longings from China, only to find his stuff intermingled
with Shane's.

After finishing the thirty reps, he dropped the weights
with a clatter then sat back with a sigh.

He really was grateful to be alive. For a moment, he
stared at his hand and the three fingers numb from
nerve damage. What in the hell was he going to do if
the damaged muscles didn't heal well enough for him
to return to the operating room? His goal all through
med school had been to become a trauma surgeon.
Yeah, there were plenty of other specialties out there,
but he didn't want to consider anything else. He closed
the fingers into a fist. His hand might be getting better,
he'd managed to intubate Abby's patient, but the
simple procedure didn't take nearly as much finesse as
surgery did.

As usual, he didn't want to dwell on the bleak thoughts.

Abby's dire summation of the rehab doctor's practice
came back to him. His specialty wasn't physical
medicine, but he knew very well that the standard of
care for rehab wasn't that much different from any other
medical service. Physicians were expected to see their
patients in the hospital on a regular basis.

If Abby was correct, Roland wasn't even meeting the
minimum requirement dictated by his profession.

Nick stood and slowly made his way across the
physical therapy gym. Pretty sad when his toughest
decision of the day was whether or not he should shower
here or return to his motel room across the street. With
a snort, he chose the privacy of his motel room.

"Are you finished, Dr Tremayne?" The physical therapist, Paul, stopped him before he reached the doorway.

"Yeah, for now. I'll probably be back tomorrow, though."

"No problem. I'll be here," Paul assured him.

Nick was about to leave, then he turned back. "There's a doctor here by the name of Roland who works on the rehab unit."

Paul's eyebrows raised up. "You mean the medical director of Rehab?"

Medical director? How could a guy who didn't make routine rounds be the medical director of the unit? Nick swallowed his surprise. Had Abby exaggerated Roland's lax attitude? From what little he knew of her, she didn't seem the type to overstate the truth.

"I guess that's the guy. What's his first name?"

"Douglas." If Paul was curious about his question, he didn't show it. Probably figured with his messed-up body, Nick was asking for personal reasons, like seeking a new doctor.

If what Abby said was true, Roland would be last on his list if he did.

"Douglas Roland," he repeated. The name wasn't familiar, but he committed it to memory. There were dozens of veterans' hospitals across the nation. There was no reason for him to know the guy, although he had worked in several of them. "Thanks."

He'd use the hospital computer system, another government perk, to check the guy out and see what information he could find.

Hell, anything was better than sitting around, feeling useless.

A few hours later Nick didn't have many concrete answers. He'd made himself at home in the hospital library, using the computer to find out what he could about standards of practice regarding MD rounds. The only thing he'd learned for certain was that rehab was a step down from acute care and, as he'd figured, the physician was only expected to make rounds every two days.

Abby had a right to be concerned about the care her patients received, though. He wished there was something more he could do to help.

He did a search and found Roland's boss, the chief of staff, listed as a Dr Rick Johnson. There was also an opening for a temporary consultant in the department of physical medicine. He stared at the advertisement for a long time. Interesting. Maybe he could fill in for a while, to give him something constructive to do and perhaps help out Abby at the same time? Of course, he'd have to run that idea past his boss back in Virginia first. Somehow he didn't think Stephen White would mind. Before he could change his mind and chicken out, he placed a call to his boss but Stephen wasn't in so he left a message.

Turning his attention back to the computer, he did another search on Dr Douglas Roland. All he found out was that he had apparently been at the hospital here in Milwaukee for the past six years, the last two as the medical director. How the guy had managed to get promoted was a mystery. Unless he'd only gone slack once he'd reached the top position.

After glancing at his watch, Nick realized the time was already well after noon. Abby's shift probably ended at three so he could grab something to eat in the hospital cafeteria, then wander up to the rehab unit to find her.

Anticipation tightened his gut even though he knew better than to think of Abby on a personal level. She was far too good for him and a great nurse. That morning she'd been all business, her grave expression betraying her genuine concern for her patient. He'd gathered from her letters how seriously she took her responsibilities, which was the main reason he'd expected someone older.

One of my patients died three days after we discharged him home. He took his own life, Shane. I can't stop thinking about it. I should have looked harder to find some sign of depression. I even went back into the system to review all the nursing notes, but I wasn't the only one who missed it, we all did. Or maybe we simply didn't want to see how depressed he was, I don't know. There is no way to go back and fix things now, but his death weighs heavily on my conscience.

For some reason, her brief story stayed with him. Maybe because he could relate to the depression the kid must have felt. With the help of Abby's letter, he had been able to recognize his own feelings and fight off the black cloud when it loomed too close.

He was glad she didn't have any clue how much he'd hung on her every word.

The cafeteria wasn't too crowded, but he almost dropped his tray on the floor when he tried to balance the thing with one hand while leaning on his cane with the other. He managed to set the tray down on the nearest vacant table, but his chest burned with pent-up frustration. He was barely self-sufficient. How much longer would he have to limp around before he'd be back to his normal self?

Maybe never.

Bile rose into his throat and he forced it back with several deep breaths. No, he refused to believe the worst. He was truly thankful for his life, but was it so wrong to want his old career back?

Ignoring the few hospital employees seated at various tables around him, he concentrated on swallowing each bite of his food without tasting a thing. Protein equaled strength, and strength would lead to building and repairing his muscle mass. He didn't dare miss a meal, no matter how much he didn't feel like eating. He pushed away the haunting thoughts about his career and focused on what he needed to do to get through the day.

The hour was close to three when he finally made his way upstairs. He'd stopped at the information desk in the lobby to find out where the rehab unit was located. He figured it wouldn't be too far from the physical therapy gym and, in fact, the unit was located just one floor up.

He didn't see Abby in the hallway, but the familiar clinical scent stopped him dead. Damn. Hospitals always carried the strong smell of antiseptic, but this was different. The scent of urine was stronger here, probably because many of the patients were elderly and unable to take care of the most basic of needs.

His hand tightened on his cane. A few short weeks ago, he'd been one of them.

Forcing himself to move, he headed down the long hall toward the nurses' station. He saw a few patients, mostly men, sitting in wheelchairs in the dining room. But he didn't see anyone from the nursing staff.

Then he realized why. Change of shift meant nurses were giving reports to each other, transferring care. He stood awkwardly, feeling stupid and trying not to dwell on the horrible memories of being a patient himself.

All his instincts shouted at him to leave, to get the hell out of there before someone realized they'd made a mistake by discharging him too soon and tossed him back into a hospital bed.

He licked dry lips and tried to remind himself he was a doctor, not a patient. He'd have to get used to being in the hospital environment as a physician, and put those painful memories of being a patient aside once and for all. Better to start now in a different rehab unit than the one he'd spent time in.

Despite his internal pep talk, standing amidst the rehab patients was one of the hardest things he'd ever had to do.

Abby finished her report, then walked out toward the front of the desk. Now that her shift was over, she wanted to head over to the ICU to check on Mr Goetz. During her lunch break, she'd gone to see him but he'd been down in Radiology, having a MRI scan of his head. All day, she'd wondered how he was doing.

"Hi, Abby."

She glanced up, surprised to see Nick standing on the opposite side of the nurses' station. Her pulse kicked up a notch when she drank in the sight of him, but she tried to sound casual. "Hi. What are you doing up here?"

"Just being nosy, I guess. Do you have a minute to show me around the unit?" Nick held her gaze with his.

A part of her wanted to refuse. She needed, for the sake of her sanity, to check on Mr Goetz, but if there was any chance Nick could help her get someone's attention about Dr Roland, she decided she'd better take it.

"Sure. Just give me a minute to grab my purse." She turned back to the report room and fetched her purse out of her locker. Then she rounded the desk and approached him. As he had that first night, he stood painfully straight, holding onto his cane. Up close, the tangy scent of his aftershave teased her senses. She almost leaned toward him to inhale deeply, then pulled herself up short. What was wrong with her? She cleared her throat. "We have a thirty-bed rehab unit." Abby gestured to one hallway. "The brain-injury patients are normally housed in the center wing, the musculo-skeletal injuries are on the right."

Nick frowned. "What happens if one of the head-injury patients wanders off?"

"We have alarms that sound if a patient leaves the unit unattended," she assured him. "We use the wander-guard system. Trust me, we know if anyone leaves the unit."

Impressed, he nodded. "Good."

"The dining room is at the end of this hall." She headed down that way, although there weren't too many patients seated in the dining area so early. "We think it's good for them to get out of their rooms to eat in a common place."

"Hmm." Nick's shrug was noncommittal and she wondered what he'd thought of the practice when he'd been a patient. His familiarity with rehab was obvious. What sort of a patient had he been? She imagined patience wasn't his greatest personality strength.

"This is a nice area, but I noticed the third wing is completely empty. Why haven't you moved the physical therapy gym to this floor, too? Wouldn't that be more convenient for the patients?"

"Yes, it would." She could only sigh. "We suggested that very thing a while ago, but I guess the planned renovation didn't survive the budget cuts." Roland's new office had survived, complete with cherrywood furniture and floor-to-ceiling bookcases, but not the relocation of the gym. She didn't want to keep bashing Dr Roland but, honestly, with him in charge, it seemed nothing happened to facilitate better patient care.

"Roland isn't around, I take it?" he asked, as if he'd read her uncharitable thoughts.

"No." She turned back, leading the way toward the main nurses' station. Thinking about Roland would only make her mad.

"Is your shift over?" Nick wanted to know as they walked off the rehab unit.

She thought about how he must feel, being in a strange city all alone. Despite her annoyance with the way he'd read her letters, she couldn't manage to stay angry with him. The idea of Nick sitting in his tiny motel room for the rest of the evening bothered her.

"Yes, I'm off, thank goodness." She flashed him a quick smile. "You know, my dad would be thrilled if you'd come over for dinner again," she offered. "I know you're probably sick of his incessant questions, but if you're not too busy, we'd love to have you."

Dazed, Nick shook his head. "I know your parents were close to Shane, but he wasn't their son. I'm not sure I understand why your dad is so interested."

Abby suspected she'd gotten her longing for adventure from her dad. He'd always wanted to travel too, but there wasn't much sightseeing you could do while carting around six kids whose ages spanned eleven years. She didn't want to go into all that detail, so she gave Nick the shortened version.

"Shane was around all the time when he and Adam were younger. Then his parents moved out of state while he and Adam were still in high school. Shane moved in for two years until he graduated. Then he and Adam both went to college in Madison for pre-med."

Nick raised a brow. "I didn't realize your brother was a physician, too."

"Yes, but he specializes in pediatrics." Abby glanced at the clock, then gestured to the elevator. "What do you think? Will you come for dinner?"

A shadow passed over his gaze, then quickly disappeared. "Why not?"

"Great. First, though, I need to stop over in the ICU."

"To see Mr Goetz," Nick guessed.

"Yep."

They rode the elevator to the fourth floor. The ICU was on the other side of the building, so she headed down the hall, slowing her pace to accommodate his lopsided gait. "I tried to see Mr Goetz earlier but he was having an MRI scan. I hope he's doing all right."

"I'm curious to see how he's faring, too."

"What do you think caused his seizure?" she asked.

"Hard to say." Nick shrugged his good shoulder. "Could be anything from a brain tumor to a stroke. A stroke is a common complication of hip surgery. But, either way, the MRI will tell them what they need to know."

Abby fell silent as they approached the ICU. She'd never worked there, and she found the environment intimidating. Nick didn't seem to notice her apprehension, and pushed the button on the wall that opened the automatic doors. She could just imagine what an imposing picture he would make as the trauma surgeon in charge. She fought the urge to step back. He was way out of her league.

The unit clerk behind the main desk raised her head when they entered. "Hello, may I help you?"

Abby stepped forward with determination. "Yes, we'd like to see Mr Goetz, if you don't mind. I'm his nurse from the rehab unit."

"Oh, uh, OK. Just a minute." The unit clerk appeared flustered as she reached for the phone. "Mary? The floor nurse is here to see your patient in bed twelve."

"Something's wrong," Nick murmured beside her. "His name isn't on the board."

What board? Abby didn't understand, then she saw it, the main census board for the unit. As her gaze traveled down the list of names, the warning knot in her stomach tightened like a noose.

An older nurse, wearing scrubs, came over toward them. "Hi, my name is Mary. I understand you're here to see Mr Goetz."

"Yes. I was his nurse on the rehab floor and witnessed his seizure. Is he OK? Did you transfer him to the general floor already?"

"No, I'm sad to say Mr Goetz died about an hour ago."

Abby grabbed for Nick and his hand closed with a reassuring strength around hers as the nurse continued. "We did the MRI and found a large mass. They wanted to take him directly to the OR to remove it, but he suffered a cardiac arrest before they could get him there. Considering his prognosis with the brain tumor, there wasn't anything more we could do." She shrugged helplessly. "I'm sorry."

CHAPTER FIVE

FOR a horrible moment Nick wondered if Abby was going to faint. He should have known better, she was made of sterner stuff than that. Her hand clutched his as if it was a lifeline, but she remained calm. His admiration for her rose another notch.

"Thanks for letting me know." Abby's voice held a slight waver.

"You're welcome. I just wish we had better news." With an apologetic smile, the ICU nurse hurried off.

"Come on, we need to get out of here." Nick tried to edge her toward the door, wishing there were something he could do to ease her pain.

"I made him go to therapy. He said he was too tired and I made him go," she whispered. "What kind of nurse am I?"

He was all too familiar with the confused feelings ricocheting through her head. Hadn't he been there himself four months ago? Guilt was a powerful emotion.

"A great nurse, Abby." He spoke firmly. "The brain tumor didn't grow overnight," he pointed out. "He could have just as easily had his seizure during breakfast as during physical therapy."

"I know." Her tone lacked conviction.

Somehow he managed to get her out of the ICU and down the hall to the waiting room. There, he stopped and pulled her close with his good arm. "Are you really all right?"

She leaned into his embrace. The warm vanilla scent of her helped him ignore the flash of pain from the added stress on his leg. "Yeah. I think so," she muttered against him.

Inappropriate as it was, he couldn't help reveling in the softness of her body pressed against his, from the curve of her breast to the slope of her hip. The sensation was all too brief, as she pulled away a few moments later.

"Let's get out of here." Her voice was stronger now.

"Only if you're all right." He didn't mind giving her the time she needed to grieve for her patient.

"I'm fine. Still upset about Roland's lack of attention to his patients, but otherwise fine."

Nick hesitated, feeling compelled to point out the truth. "Even if Roland had made rounds and had known about Mr Goetz's headaches, chances are he wouldn't have ordered any additional treatment. Brain tumors are extremely hard to diagnose without more severe symptoms. It's not like every person with a headache gets an MRI scan."

Abby let out a long breath. "I know. In here..." she tapped her skull "...I do understand, you're right. We all make jokes about it, saying stuff like, 'I have a headache.

Gee, hope it's not a brain tumor.' But I still worry Mr Goetz might have had other symptoms we missed."

"Maybe, but maybe not." Nick longed to reach for her again, but forced himself to keep his hands to himself. "Don't dwell on this, Abby. You did the best you could with the information you had."

"I'll try not to." She offered a lopsided smile, although the sheen of tears still glistened in her eyes.

"Good. You ready to go?" When she nodded, Nick steered her toward the elevators with a gentle hand on the small of her back. The heat of her skin seemed to sear the tips of his fingers. Why he had this sudden awareness for a woman after all these months was beyond him. Especially a woman who deserved someone better than him. Once he'd been focused on his career, then on getting back on his feet. This hard-edged need for Abby didn't factor into his plans. He tried to think of something to distract him from his crazy thoughts. "Do you want to walk the couple of blocks to your parents' house?"

"Sure."

They took the elevator down to the first-floor lobby, but once outside Abby halted in mid-stride.

"Wait a minute. I'd rather stop at your motel room first."

He nearly tripped over his cane and his heart jack-hammered in his chest. Did she really mean what he thought she did? What he secretly hoped she did? He was sure he was staring at her in shock and had to remind himself to breathe. "You do?"

"Yes." Abby sent him an impatient glance. "I refuse

to walk all the way to my parents' without getting your medication first. Last night you were in so much pain, you could barely make it home."

The balloon of his ego deflated. Had he really thought she might be interested in a quick romp in his motel room? He'd laugh if he didn't feel so stupid. Idiot, he thought as he pulled himself together. The truth was, Abby cared about making sure he wasn't in pain. Which was nice, but didn't top the list of things he wanted from a woman.

What he had in mind was likely to cause more physical discomfort, but he didn't care. And he didn't want his woman worrying about anything other than pleasure either.

"Ah, well." He cleared his throat and glanced across the street to where his motel was located. "You can wait here if you like. I won't be long." Maybe there would be time for a cold shower.

"Oh, I'd rather walk with you." Abby didn't take his giant hint, but fell into step beside him. She lifted her face toward the sky and closed her eyes. "The sun feels so good."

Nick glanced away, far too tempted to kiss her. Just one taste, to help combat the constant pain. "Yeah, it does. Summertime in Wisconsin is pretty nice."

"Where did you grow up, Nick?" she asked, as they waited for a break in traffic before crossing the street.

"Chicago." He wasn't trying to be evasive, but his past wasn't a cheerful topic of discussion. "Heck, Chicago isn't all that far from Milwaukee. We were practically neighbors."

She chuckled. Before she could ask anything further, though, he forestalled her by asking a few questions of his own. "What happened to your mother? I think it's great the way you and your siblings have pulled together to help her."

"She got tangled with Murphy, took a header down the stairs and broke her hip. Because of our medical background, Adam and I have taken on most of Mom's personal care, including going to all her doctor's appointments. Alaina has taken over the household chores, with some help from Alec when he's not working at hauling in the bad guys. He's a cop." She frowned. "Dad tries to help with Mom, but he isn't as young as he used to be either."

He unlocked the door to his hotel room and hoped she'd continue to talk so he wouldn't have time to think about the kiss they'd shared the night before. Had it really been only twenty-four hours ago? It didn't seem possible. Abby fell silent.

"Give me a minute to get my stuff." He took refuge in the bathroom.

The pill bottles lined up along the edge of the sink gave him pause. Damn. He'd bet Abby's elderly mother didn't have as many prescriptions as he did. Resentment flared, hot and slick. He was tempted to swipe the whole bunch into the toilet and flush them away.

Only the memory of how hard it had been to use the weight machine earlier stopped him. As much as he detested his physical limitations, he wasn't so sure he'd be able to get himself out of bed in the morning without the stupid pills.

He was weaning himself off them, slowly but surely. He was down to three times a day and, hopefully, soon he'd only need them in the morning and then again at night.

He opened and closed his hand again, trying to fight off a sense of panic. He refused to think the worst. His hand and his leg were getting better every day.

Maybe.

Swearing under his breath, he grabbed his pain meds off the bathroom sink, stuffed a few in his pants pocket, then slammed the bottle back down before going out to find Abby.

She turned from the window when he entered the room. Some of his self-loathing evaporated when he was struck by how the sun brightened her hair, like a halo.

Time to get out of his motel room with its oversized bed dominating the room.

"Let's go." He crossed the room and opened the door.

Abby fell into step beside him. They hadn't walked very far when the sound of music filled the air.

"Listen!" Abby grabbed his hand, her blue eyes bright with excitement. "Do you hear that? There's a park just one block over. Come on, I bet there's a band playing there." She tugged on him, intent on changing their course, then just as abruptly stopped. "Oh, I'm sorry. I forgot about your leg. We don't need to go."

"I'm fine." He was irritated by her hesitation, but knew she couldn't help her nursing instincts. He tried to smile. "Walking is good for it. And the music is a nice way to relax after a stressful day."

"Yes, it is." A shadow fell over her eyes and he figured she was thinking about Mr Goetz. "Are you sure?" She paused, then, when he nodded, she headed down the street.

"You must be a fan of jazz." He followed her lead.

Her lips curved in a lopsided smile. "Yeah. Jazz was also Shane's favorite."

The kernel of guilt returned, nagging like a sore tooth. Should he tell her what had happened? No matter how much she deserved the truth, he didn't know if he could bear seeing the innocent expression on her face turn to disgust once she knew how Shane had died.

Especially when he should have been the one to die instead.

No one would have really mourned his loss if he had, except maybe his boss. No family, no girlfriend, no kids. He had spent his life doing anything he liked without ties to anyone.

Self-centered? You bet. Self-centered was his middle name.

There was a good-sized crowd gathered in the park as the four-piece jazz band belted out some good old-fashioned blues.

The neighborhood gathering was very different from what he'd grown up with in Chicago. Milwaukee was a fairly large city, but this seemed more like something you'd find in a small town.

Abby tapped her foot in time to the music and he imagined she loved to dance. He set his jaw. His leg didn't hold up to walking, much less dancing. No matter how determined he was to comply with his therapy, he often wondered if he'd ever get back to normal.

His cell phone rang, and he flipped it open when he

recognized his boss's number, plugging one ear so he could hear better. "Tremayne."

"Got your message, Nick." Stephen White's booming voice was easy to hear, especially since the band chose that moment to take a break. "I think it's a good idea for you to try out the temporary consultant position. I might be able to create a full-time consultant job here in Virginia if you decide to go that route, but I'll have to free up another position first."

"I don't know about that." The idea of doing something more permanent didn't sit well with him, he wasn't ready to give up being a surgeon. A temporary position was just that, temporary.

"Your decision," Stephen agreed. "See how it goes. But for now, get in touch with the chief of staff, Rick Johnson. I'll give you a recommendation if you need one."

"Thanks. I'll find Johnson first thing in the morning," Nick promised.

"Good, good. How are you doing?" Stephen asked, and Nick knew his boss's question was aimed at getting information about him on a personal level.

"Excellent," Nick lied. He had no intention of whining to his boss and mentor about his physical problems. From the way Stephen had offered to create a different role for him, he figured his boss wasn't altogether confident he'd make it back to the operating room either. "I'm sorry, Stephen, but I gotta go. I'll let you know what happens after I talk to Johnson."

"All right. Goodbye."

Nick snapped his phone shut, feeling a surge of anticipation he hadn't felt in a long time. Tomorrow he'd talk to Johnson about the job. Pathetic to be so excited about a consultant position, especially a temporary one. But at least this way he might be able to help out Abby. If the unit's medical director really wasn't doing his job, then he'd be in a position to do something about it.

Abby's eyes were bright with curiosity. "What was that all about? Johnson? As in the chief of staff—that Dr Johnson?"

Slowly Nick nodded. The crowd around them had thinned with the band's break, so they continued to walk toward Abby's parents' house. "Yeah, there's a temporary consultant position open on the rehab unit. I thought maybe I could fill in for a little while and see how things are running up there. My boss gave me the go-ahead to discuss the position with Johnson."

"Really?" Her expression turned hopeful.

He grimaced. "It's not exactly as if I'm overwhelmingly busy at the moment."

"I'm so glad." Relief relaxed her tense features. "After the way Roland spoke to me the other day, I can't wait to see how he behaves with a new physician around."

He frowned. "What did he say to you?"

"It doesn't matter." She waved him off with a hand. "I was rude first. It got me a note on my file, but it was worth it."

"Wait a minute. Your file? What on earth happened?"

Now her ivory cheeks were tinged pink. "Nothing. I told you, I was rude first."

This time it was her cell phone that rang. Irritated,

she opened it up. "I'm on my way, Alaina. Tell Mom not to worry."

When she'd finished her call, he glanced at her. "I'm going to keep bugging you until you tell me what happened."

She rolled her eyes. "All right, if you must know, I paged him several times about Mr Goetz."

"And?" he asked when she paused.

"And, when he finally called back four hours later, he acted as if I'd paged him for nothing."

From what he knew of Abby, he couldn't imagine she'd paged the guy for nothing. "Jerk."

"Exactly." She grinned. "So I asked him if he'd bother responding to his page next time."

Nick chuckled. "Good for you."

"Yeah, well, the nurse working with me was horrified and the nursing director wasn't too thrilled with me either. Most of the nurses I work with are either brand-new and too afraid to speak up or they've been there for ever and don't want to make any waves. I don't get it. It's the patients who are suffering."

Abby led the way up the stairs of her parents' front porch. Nick heard her father call out before they even reached the door.

"Abby? Is that you?"

"Yes, Dad. And guess what? I convinced Nick to come for dinner again." She sent Nick a teasing smile that kicked his pulse into triple digits.

"Great, bring him in, then. Nick, what can I get you to drink?" Abe greeted Nick as if he didn't already have four sons of his own.

"Whatever you're having is fine." Nick stood in the living room across from the massive wall of pictures and wondered if this sensation of coming home was how Shane had felt. For a moment he felt paralyzed.

Shane had saved his life, and now he himself had stolen Shane's place as the adopted son of the Monroe household. Worse, he wanted Shane's woman.

Could he sink any lower?

Abby raced upstairs to find her mother had already gotten herself washed and dressed, and was working on combing her wet hair.

Guilt wrenched her. "Mom, I'm so sorry I'm late. Why didn't you wait for me?"

"You were the one telling me I need to start doing things for myself," Alice reminded her. "So don't get mad when I take your advice."

"I'm not mad at all, just worried." She eased the brush from her mom's hand then went to work on the tangles. "So how did it go? You didn't slip or anything, did you?"

"I didn't actually take a bath, just sat in a chair and showered," her mother admitted. "Getting in and out was hard enough, even with the help of a chair."

Abby momentarily closed her eyes. Thank heavens her mother hadn't fallen. Instead of coming straight home after work, she'd dawdled with Nick. To her dismay, she'd constantly relived the exciting moment of his kiss, longing for a repeat performance.

She really had to stop daydreaming about the man. He wasn't interested in her, for one thing. Hadn't he been the one who had pulled away after that first kiss?

And, besides, she didn't like the way her mind constantly compared him to Shane, especially when Shane was the one who came up lacking.

Which was ridiculous. Shane had been a great friend and a wonderful doctor. He'd fit perfectly into the Monroe family. He hadn't been the least bit arrogant, as she suspected Nick had probably been before his injury.

She helped her mother negotiate the stairs, wondering what Nick and her father were talking about. A wry laugh escaped. Oh, yeah, she had it bad. Hadn't she just told herself to get over him? What was wrong with her? She hadn't felt this excited about seeing Shane when he'd hung around.

Maybe because Nick was an unknown entity. Once she'd gotten to know him better, she wouldn't feel like this about him any more.

In the kitchen, Alec and Alaina were making dinner. Or, rather, Alaina was doing most of the work, while Alec directed activities from his chair.

"It's about time you showed up." Alec scowled. "Mom was worried. Did you have to work late?"

Gritting her teeth, she smiled at him. "What's the matter, Alec? Cranky because you didn't catch any bad guys last night?"

He ignored her dig. "What's with this Nick guy you're seeing?" he wanted to know. "Fill me in."

"I'm not seeing him," she denied. "He's a friend, just here for a simple dinner."

"Again?" Alaina wagged her eyebrows. "Hmm."

"Oh, stop it." This was why she wanted to leave, so she could simply live her life without having to deal with the constant opinions of her nosy family. Abby peered over Alaina's shoulder. "Your chicken salad looks good."

"Thanks." Alaina swiped her hands on a towel, then handed her the bowl. "You can carry this to the dining room."

She swallowed the automatic protest and did as she was told. From the dining room, she could hear Nick and her father talking outside on the porch. She paused, eavesdropping on their conversation.

"No, sir," Nick was saying. "I don't really have any family of my own. I grew up in foster homes and joined the service as soon as I graduated high school."

"How in tarnation did you manage to get into medical school?" Abe asked in an incredulous tone.

"I was lucky. They gave me a series of standard tests and realized I was brighter than my bad grades indicated." When he paused, Abby strained to listen. Nick almost sounded embarrassed. "Seems my greatest strength was science so they helped put me through college, then medical school." Nick's voice grew quieter. "I had to agree to give the government several years of my life dedicated to serving the armed forces but, all in all, I was very lucky. Without them, I wouldn't be where I am today."

Stunned, she shivered at the depth of emotion in his voice. Nick had been raised in a series of foster homes, barely graduated from high school, and he thought he was lucky.

Most surgeons were arrogant, but not Nick. Now she knew why.

"Abby?" Her father's voice rose. "Would you please bring us a refill on our lemonade?"

"Sure." She set the bowl down in the center of the dining table, then went back into the kitchen for the pitcher of lemonade. Alec stood.

"When do I get to meet him?" Alec cracked his knuckles, pretending to be tough. "Does he know I carry a gun?"

"Ha, ha. Very funny." Ignoring her brother's attempt at humor, she went outside to the porch where Nick and her father were sitting.

Her father beamed. "Thanks, sweetheart. Lord, Nick, I'll tell you, I don't know what we're going to do once Abby's gone." Her father shook his head ruefully. "We've really come to depend on her."

"Gone?" Nick's gaze swiveled toward her, a frown puckered between his brows. "You mean, like taking a well-deserved vacation?"

"Hell, no, I mean when she moves away." Abe didn't seem to notice Nick's startled expression. "Didn't she tell you? She's moving to Florida in a few weeks. Even has a job lined up down there." Abe smiled and winked at her. "Do you know how many miles are between Milwaukee and Fort Meyers, Nick? One thousand, five hundred and three."

"Dad," Abby warned. Nick's dumbfounded expression twisted her stomach into a knot.

"No." Nick's tone was clipped. "She didn't tell me." Abby didn't know what to say. She hadn't intentionally kept her plans secret. But the faint accusation in his gaze told her he thought otherwise.

CHAPTER SIX

NICK's intense gaze throughout dinner robbed Abby of her appetite. There was no reason to feel lousy about not sharing her plans with him. They barely knew each other, and certainly didn't have that sort of close relationship.

This time together was just a brief interlude in their lives. In a few days, maybe a week at the most, they'd go their separate ways. Nick would return to whatever temporary base he called home and she'd finish out her stint at the Veterans' Hospital then move to her new job in Florida.

A sense of desolation crept over her. Her plans to move had seemed like such a great idea. Her brothers had lived in different states. Nick had lived all over the world. He hadn't been tied down by an overprotective family.

So why wasn't she happier at the idea of going?

"You were stationed in Germany for a year, then?" Abe asked Nick. "How did you manage, without speaking the language?"

Nick shrugged as if embarrassed by all the attention

to his past. "I picked up some of the language along the way. It's not as hard as you might think." Then he grimaced, and added, "Except for Chinese. Talk about a difficult language to figure out. The whole time in Beijing, I didn't learn much more than the words for hello, goodbye and bathroom."

Abby picked at her food, wishing the meal would end soon. Her parents listened to Nick with rapt attention. Strange, Shane had been so much a part of the family that her parents hadn't acted as if him being around had been anything special. She found the way they fawned over Nick irritating.

Finally she stood up and began clearing the table.

"Anyone want dessert?" her mother asked.

"Thank you, but I'm full." Nick smiled.

"Yeah," Alec agreed. "Me, too."

"Why don't you go sit on the porch for a while? It's a beautiful evening," Abby encouraged her parents. "We'll save your peach cobbler for later."

Her parents headed outside and Alaina went in search of her children. Alec sat for a minute at the table, but when Nick stood and pitched in to help with the dishes, her brother made a quick escape. Apparently, his desire to keep an eye on Nick lost over the threat of having to wash dishes.

Nick's movements were slow and stiff, making Abby wonder if he'd taken the medication they'd stopped to pick up.

His lopsided gait was definitely more pronounced as she followed him to the kitchen. She gave a mild snort. Yeah. Not likely.

"Where's your pain medication?" she asked, setting down her load of dishes in the sink with a clatter.

Nick scowled at her. "I'm fine." As if to prove it, he spun awkwardly around and went back to the dining room for more dishes.

Gnashing her teeth at his stubbornness, Abby began to rinse the glassware, then packed them in the dishwasher. When he returned, she took the stack of plates from his hands.

"You're not fine, Nick. I don't get it. What is the big deal with taking pain medication you so obviously need?"

"You're right. You don't get it at all." His eyes flashed and she was taken aback by his anger.

"It's all about your ego, isn't it?" She jammed the dishes into the dishwasher with far more force than necessary. He was acting just like her brothers. "Heaven forbid you should give in to any weakness."

She gasped when he spun her away from the dishwasher, and hauled her against his hard frame. Her pulse quickened with anticipation.

"No, it's not about my ego."

This close his gray-green eyes glittered with flecks of gold around his dilated pupils. She splayed her hands over his chest, the muscles taut beneath her fingertips. She wished she could touch his bare skin, even though she knew she was already playing with fire.

"Those pills create a foggy haze in my mind I detest. At least feeling the jagged edges of pain helps remind me I'm alive." His gaze lingered on her mouth and his voice dropped low. "Reminds me that being here like this, with you and your family, isn't a damn dream, that

I won't wake up to find myself strapped in some strange hospital bed."

Shaken, she stared at him. What horrors he must have gone through. The unguarded emotion in his gaze called to her on a completely different level. Unable to help herself, Abby rose on tiptoe and pressed her lips against his. At first he seemed startled by her kiss, then in an instant he yanked her close and delved deep, as if he were a dying man given his last sip of water.

Then, just as abruptly, he pushed her away, his chest heaving as if he'd run ten miles. Without his arms supporting her, she stumbled back against the edge of the sink, dazed and wondering what had just happened.

"This isn't smart. I have to go." He limped away surprisingly fast and she couldn't do anything except listen as he said thanks and bade her parents goodnight before he left.

She closed her eyes and rubbed a hand over her forehead. As much as she was sick and tired of his pull-me, push-me routine, one thing she could agree with.

Kissing him was not at all smart.

Abby worked a couple of night shifts, then was more than happy to have a few days off. On her second day off, however, the shrill ringing of the phone woke her. She opened one bleary eye to see the hour was barely six. As much as she wanted to bury her head under the pillow, there could only be one place calling so early.

She snagged the phone by the third ring. "Hello?"

"Abby? This is the night supervisor at the hospital. We had a sick call this morning, would you mind coming in?"

Heck, yeah, she minded, but bit back the automatic refusal. The extra money would come in handy when she moved. And she couldn't bear to think of the patients suffering while the nurses worked short-handed. Repressing a sigh, she agreed. "Yes, but I might be a little late."

"Thanks so much, Abby. You're a lifesaver." The night supervisor quickly hung up before she could change her mind.

A shower helped clear the sleepy fog from her brain. Thanks to Nick, sleep hadn't come easily. In an effort to avoid dwelling on her irrational feelings for Nick, she'd tried to remember some of the happy times she'd had with Shane. But for some reason she'd had trouble picturing Shane's image, until at midnight she'd crawled from her bed to dig out an old photo to help build a clearer picture in her mind.

Even then, most of her memories were centered around times they'd hung out as a family. Like when they'd all played tackle football the day after Thanksgiving. She, Shane and Adam had been on the same team. When Shane had lobbed a pass at her, she'd caught it for the winning touchdown. He'd run after her, nearly tackling her in the process of enveloping her in a big hug to celebrate.

Shane had been a known entity, but Nick wasn't. Abby finished putting on her scrubs, then grabbed her stethoscope and headed outside to walk the few blocks to work. It had been distressing to realize how few times she and Shane had actually been alone. Truthfully, even the kiss he'd given her before leaving for Beijing was difficult to recall. Nick's searing, demanding kisses were so different, so clearly vivid in her mind, overshadowing her memories of Shane.

A fact she didn't like one bit. With a frown, she picked up her pace, knowing the later she was, the longer the night nurse would have to stay overtime.

Luckily hard work had the great advantage of distracting her from thoughts of Nick Tremayne.

Just before lunch, one of the floors called to give report on a patient who had been accepted as a rehab transfer. Abby volunteered to take the new admission and asked one of the patient care aides to get a room ready while she finished hanging an IV antibiotic.

The patient was rolled in a half-hour later. The floor nurse had informed her the patient was Gerald Fischer, a 73-year-old man recovering from an ischemic stroke, the type caused by a blood clot. Abby entered his room with a bright smile. "Good morning, Mr Fischer. How are you feeling?"

"Purple shoe. Shoe, purple shoe."

What? His earnest, compelling gaze convinced her he wasn't trying to be funny. She stepped closer, noticing how the pupil in his right eye was slightly larger than his left.

"Mr Fischer, squeeze my fingers with your hands." Abby tried not to show her concern, but she was worried he'd extended his stroke. Or his stroke hadn't resolved in the first place. How on earth had he been accepted for transfer?

He took her fingers and squeezed, but his right side was markedly weaker than his left. When she continued her assessment, she found he couldn't move his right leg at all.

"I'm going to call the doctor, Mr Fischer. Don't get out of bed by yourself, all right? Use this call-light here if you need something. I'll be right back."

Abby nabbed the patient care aide's attention as she made her way to the nurses' station. "Go and sit with Mr Fischer for a few minutes. His stroke symptoms are worse. Keep an eye on him while I call Dr Roland."

This time, when she paged Roland, she added the numbers 911 to the front of the rehab extension. If the universal code for emergency didn't get his attention, nothing would.

She took one of the unit's portable phones with her back to Mr Fischer's room, after instructing the unit secretary to forward Roland's call.

Mr Fischer wasn't any worse when she returned, but he was still babbling nonsense. She knew strokes with right-sided weakness often resulted in aphasia, a condition where the patient either couldn't speak or could only repeat the same words over and over. Inside Mr Fischer's head, he knew what he wanted to say, but because of the brain injury surrounding the stroke he couldn't make his mouth speak the words.

She could only imagine how frustrated he must feel. "Mr Fischer, I called the doctor to come and evaluate you. Did your speech recently get worse? Squeeze my hand once for yes, twice for no."

Giving only two non-speaking options was the best way to communicate with an aphasic patient. Mr Fischer squeezed her hand once.

She continued asking questions, trying to figure out exactly what had happened. If his stroke symptoms were so bad, why on earth had the floor transferred him? Surely he couldn't tolerate three hours of therapy per day? She wasn't a stroke expert, but she suspected he needed acute care and treatment.

Time was of the essence.

Her portable phone rang. She picked it up. "This is Abby."

"Roland. You paged? Again?"

She ignored his biting sarcasm. "Yes, I'm here with Mr Fischer and I'm very concerned he may have extended his stroke. He's aphasic, with a mild hand-grasp on the right compared to a strong hand-grasp on the left. He can't lift his right leg at all and his pupils are unequal. His blood pressure is 162 over 90, pulse is 104, respirations at 16. He's not running a fever."

"He doesn't sound that much worse than when I accepted his transfer," Dr Roland commented. He spoke so fast, he slurred some of his words together.

He'd actually accepted this patient with the severity of these symptoms? She moved to the doorway, trying to get out of Mr Fischer's earshot. "Dr Roland, Mr Fischer is not a candidate for rehab. I'm not even sure he can be safely cared for on a general floor. His neuro status isn't close to being stable."

"I'll take care of it. And watch your tone, or I'll write you up for insubordination," he warned, before discon-necting the call.

Open-mouthed, she stared at the phone in shock. Insubordination? For asking a doctor to come and see her patient?

"Unbelievable!" Abby resisted the urge to bang her

phone against the wall, imaging she was aiming for Roland's face. Taking a deep breath, she tried to remain calm. Roland had said he'd take care of things, but what did that mean? She hadn't detected a sense of urgency in his voice and Mr Fischer didn't have time to spare. She needed a plan B. Normally, only physicians could make referrals to other physicians, but she wasn't above stretching the truth a bit to get care for her patient.

Marching to the nurses' station, she asked Betty, the unit secretary, which doctor was on call for Neurology. Before she could change her mind, she placed a page to Dr Sue Glasner.

When the Dr Glasner called back moments later, Abby chose her words carefully. "I just got off the phone with Dr Roland, our rehab medical director, who is currently out of the hospital but making his way in. We have a patient with an ischemic stroke by the name of Mr Fischer. I don't know if your stroke team has seen him, but we're concerned he has extended his injury. Do you have time to come up and evaluate him?"

"Sure, I'll be there in fifteen minutes." The neurologist didn't question her consult and Abby hung up with a sigh of relief. OK, technically, she hadn't lied. And as long as someone came to see poor Mr Fischer, she didn't care.

Although implying that Roland had consulted the neurologist had been wrong. She scowled at the computerized chart, making a note about the call to Dr Glasner.

"Abby? What's wrong?"

She glanced up with a guilty look to find Nick standing beside her, wearing a white lab coat with a new Veterans' Hospital ID tag. He'd apparently secured the

temporary consultant position in record time. She hadn't
seen him since the dinner at her parents' house and he
looked incredible dressed in a shirt and tie. His smile
was enough to steal her breath away. "Oh—nothing.
Just one of my patients isn't doing very well."

"Which patient?"

"Mr Fischer in room 10." When Nick headed in that
direction, she picked up her scribbled notes about Mr
Fischer and hurried after him. "Where are you going?
I've already been in touch with Dr Glasner, the neurologist, she's on her way to see him."

"Excellent." Nick didn't even ask about Roland.
Abby wasn't sure if that was good or bad. "While we're
waiting I'll do a consult on the patient myself."

Nick slid into his physician role amazingly well. He
began a thorough assessment on Mr Fischer and when
Dr Glasner joined them shortly afterwards, they
compared notes on what they'd found.

"Definitely has acute symptoms," Nick told the pretty
neurologist, who was petite, with straight dark hair that
reached her jaw. A flicker of jealousy caught Abby off
guard when the two of them stood close, hovering over
the computer where Mr Fischer's chart was stored,
debating the plan of care.

*Stop being an idiot. Just because they look so good
together is no reason to barge between them like some
psycho-woman.*

"Abby, we need a CT scan of his head, stat." Nick
was looking at her oddly. "The order has been entered
into the system, all we need is for someone to call down
to Radiology."

"Of course." After giving herself a quick mental slap, she hurried out to the unit secretary to relay the request. Enough mooning over Nick. They had patients to take care of. "Betty? Call down to Radiology for an urgent CT of the head on Mr Fischer."

"By whose order?" A snide voice behind her had her spinning around to face Roland. He was short, in his early fifties and weighed almost two hundred pounds. He also reeked of cigarette smoke and something else she couldn't quite put her finger on. She'd always secretly debated how long he'd be in his position, considering he was a walking heart attack waiting to happen.

She raised a brow at the arrogant expression on his face. She remained calm, but lifted her chin so he wouldn't mistake her even response for cowering. "Dr Glasner, the neurologist, and Dr Tremayne are in Mr Fischer's room, examining him."

"Why, you little witch." Roland took a threatening step toward her, his hands balled into fists. She held her ground, but it wasn't easy. "Didn't I say I'd take care of it? You just couldn't wait to go behind my back, could you?"

Betty watched their interaction with wide eyes. The other staff members within hearing distance turned to stare at them, too.

"If you're referring to the way I arranged proper medical care for my patient, then, yes, I did." Abby narrowed her gaze. "I didn't tell them anything specific about you, though, so if you hurry, they'll never know you weren't planning to call a neurology consult."

"Too late for that, I think." Nick's sharp tone nearly

made her wince. For a guy who walked with a cane, he sure knew how to sneak around.

Roland didn't take the hint, but swung around to face Nick. "Who in the hell are you?"

"Dr Nick Tremayne, rehab consultant on the unit. I've been up here for the past three days, but I guess we haven't met." Nick gave Roland an assessing look. "I think you owe Ms Monroe an apology."

"I don't need this crap. I have a patient to see." Roland brushed past Nick, his action so abrupt Abby had the impression Roland had purposefully intended to knock Nick off balance. But Nick moved lightning fast and grabbed Roland's arm.

"Mr Fischer is no longer your patient." Nick's tight smile was grim. "Dr Glasner has just taken over the patient's care. And if you have an issue with that, I suggest you take it to the chief of staff."

CHAPTER SEVEN

NICK had never been so furious with a colleague in his entire life. He wasn't prone to violence, but if Roland hadn't stormed off, presumably in search of Rick Johnson, he actually might have socked the guy.

A temptation that wouldn't have done his surgeon's hands any good, but would have gone a long way in making him feel a heck of a lot better.

Pushing away his anger, he returned to Mr Fischer's room with Abby. Standing back, he watched as Abby hovered over her patient, keeping a close eye on him, alert to any changes for the worse. He was impressed with the way she'd stood her ground with Roland. At times like this she appeared so nice and sweet, but when she believed in something—look out.

He silently admitted one of the reasons he'd taken the temporary consultant's role had been to stay close to her. Oh, he still wanted to help out if there was a problem with patient care on the rehab unit. But the real reason he'd agreed to stay was far more complex.

Abby placed a gentle hand on Mr Fischer's arm and

the patient clutched it gratefully. Abby's care and compassion made her a great nurse. Of course, being organized didn't hurt either.

Her smile, though, was her best feature, lighting up her whole face and beaming warmth into a cold soul. He couldn't exactly figure out how she did it, but just being in her presence made a person feel better. Her patients no doubt loved her.

As Shane had? He rubbed a hand along the tense muscles along the back of his neck. Discovering her plans to move had sent him reeling. He could completely understand the desire to start over someplace new. Had losing Shane factored into her decision to leave?

His gut tightened with apprehension and he quickly sidelined the thought before guilt could swallow him whole. Her reasons for leaving didn't matter one way or the other. Abby needed a friend and, as much as he hated to admit it, Shane wasn't here.

But that hadn't stopped *him* from arranging things so *he* was.

A tech from Radiology brought a gurney for Mr Fischer. Nick had already let the ICU know they might need to take him after his CT scan. As much as he'd wanted to pound some sense into Roland's thick skull, Roland wasn't the physician responsible for this mess. The doctor who'd initiated the transfer off the acute unit in the first place was at fault.

He left Mr Fischer's room and headed to the nurses' station where he could use the phone to track down Mr Fischer's transferring physician. Multiple phone calls later, he'd finally gotten the information he needed.

"Did you find out why the floor transferred Mr Fischer?" Abby asked after he'd hung up the phone.

"Yeah." Nick sat back in his chair, massaging his thigh with one hand. "The hospital is in a severe bed crunch. The resident hadn't seen Mr Fischer since much earlier this morning, but heard how they had patients backed up in the ED, so he basically made the decision to request a transfer to rehab."

"And Dr Roland accepted the patient."

"Yep. According to the resident, he gave Roland the symptoms he'd noticed earlier that morning, not anything more recent. Roland went ahead and accepted the patient. As far as he knows, Roland never assessed the patient for himself."

Her brow furrowed. "Even if Roland had accepted the patient, the nurses on the floor should have recognized how much worse he was. They should have phoned the resident to stop the transfer."

Nick shrugged. "Yeah, but if they were short-staffed and knew they had to make room for other patients, they may not have taken the time to assess him very closely either."

Her smile was bittersweet. "At least he's getting the care he needs now. Thanks for supporting me with Roland."

"You're welcome." As if he possessed the willpower to stay away from her. Abby hurried off to take care of her other patients. The time she'd spent with Mr Fischer had put her behind schedule.

Watching her go, Nick berated himself for being a fool. He was already too emotionally involved with

Abby Monroe. Sharing dinner with her family and watching as she took care of her patients certainly wasn't going to help. He needed distance. Maybe taking the temporary consultant position hadn't been one of his better ideas. Being this close to Abby without touching her was killing him.

Nick sat at one of the computer workstations, glad for the chance to take some of the pressure off his leg. He finished typing his consult note on Mr Fischer into the electronic record, then reviewed Abby's documentation as well. She'd stuck to the facts, hardly implicating Roland at all. Very professional.

He stood to stretch, then reached for his stethoscope. His fingers closed around the tubing but the heavy weight of the bell pulled it from his grasp, and it fell to the floor with a clatter. He stared at the stethoscope lying in a twisted heap, then again at his numb fingers. Betrayal lodged in his throat. He'd been fooling himself. When he'd managed to intubate Abby's patient, he'd figured the nerves and muscles in his fingers were getting better. But when the stethoscope began to fall, he hadn't felt it slip from his grip.

His hand wasn't any better at all.

The nerve damage might be permanent. The nerve specialist had tried to prepare him for this, but he hadn't wanted to believe it.

Outwardly he was calm as he picked the stethoscope up from the floor, but inside impotent rage beat against his chest. He took one deep breath, then another as he walked off the unit. No use thinking about his grim future.

At least Abby had a future. She was a great nurse. She deserved to be happy, to travel wherever her heart desired. To start over and live the life of her dreams. Thinking about it now, he remembered an underlying longing in her letters to Shane, but he hadn't completely understood the depth of her feelings until now.

I have this crazy impulse to hop an international flight coming to Beijing to visit you. Your descriptions of China are so amazing. The Shanghai open market is easy to imagine, I can practically hear the people chattering in rapid-fire Chinese. I'm dying to see everything for myself. Or at least to see something outside of Wisconsin. Yet at the same time the thought of traveling alone halfway across the world is a little intimidating. I'd do it, though, for a chance to see China with you.

The idea of traveling halfway around the world hadn't bothered him at all. Once he would have been more than anxious to drop everything and take off for a new adventure.

But not any more.

Months of rehab, lying in his bed writhing in agony with no one to turn to other than the nurse currently assigned to him, had changed his whole perception on life. Thrill-seeking definitely lacked appeal.

Not that he'd gone sky-diving from planes, or bungy-jumping off cliffs, but his entire lifestyle, from the time he had been a kid, had been that of a nomad, moving restlessly from place to place, always seeking something new.

He was tired of wandering from place to place. The one thing he'd longed for during the time of his injury had been something he'd never had. Home. A family. A partner to share his life with.

For a brief moment, when he'd crossed the threshold of the Monroe household, he imagined he'd found what he had been looking for. He'd grown to care about Abby through her letters, but seeing her in person had been like touching a live wire.

She radiated positive energy in a way he envied. Under different circumstances, he'd be more than a little tempted to seduce her into his bed. He couldn't get close to her without wanting to kiss her. Yet they both stood on opposite ends of the spectrum as far as their personal lives were concerned.

He had no future as a surgeon, no idea what he'd do with the rest of his life.

Abby was well settled as a nurse, doing her best on behalf of her patients.

She devoted much of her time to her family, while Nick had lived only to please himself.

Here in Milwaukee, Nick had finally felt as if he'd come home.

And Abby had already made plans to leave.

"Are you finished for the day?" he asked when Abby finally dropped into a chair behind the nurses' station. He should have been as weary as Abby looked, but performing consults on the various rehab patients had taken his mind off his own problems. So far, he hadn't seen anything out of the ordinary with the patients' medical care.

"I think so." She sighed. "Mr Fischer was transferred

to the ICU. That makes two ICU transfers in the past week. I must be jinxed."

"You're too smart to believe in stuff like that." Nick resisted the urge to smooth a stray strand of reddish-blond hair from her cheek. She looked tired, worn out, especially after her interaction with Roland. She'd been so busy taking care of everyone else, maybe it was time for someone to take care of her? "Do you have plans for tonight?" *Smooth, Tremayne. Really smooth.*

She didn't seem to notice his poor transition from the professional to the personal. "This was supposed to be my day off." She grimaced and glanced at her watch. "Instead, I'm stuck doing an hour of overtime."

"How about if I take you out for dinner? Someplace special, like Carlo's downtown."

A flare of pleasure lit her gaze, then almost instantly faded. "Thanks, but I'm pretty tired. It's been a long day."

The way her gaze slid from his convinced him she was lying through her teeth. Initially, she'd wanted to go for dinner, then had made up the old I'm-too-tired excuse. Clearly the problem was that she didn't want to go with him.

His fault, he knew, for sending mixed signals. *Hell, his signals were so jumbled they'd been strewn throughout his body by a tornado.* They wanted different things from life, but maybe just for tonight they could find a way to meet in the middle. He just couldn't quite let her go. Besides, he wanted a chance to ask her about Roland. As long as they kept things friendly, what was the harm?

She might mess with his head, but he didn't care. He

swallowed a self-deprecating grimace. So much for thinking he'd given up his thrill-seeking behavior.

"Please?" Nick kept his voice low, although there wasn't anyone else around to overhear him. "You deserve to be pampered after the day you've put in."

She arched a brow. "Is that the only reason I should go?"

"No. You should come with me because I enjoy spending time with you." Admitting the bald truth wasn't as hard as he'd thought. Besides, whether she realized it or not, between her family and work, she needed a night away. And he wanted to be the lucky guy sharing it with her.

Abby was quiet for so long he figured he'd struck out. Again.

"So you're asking me out? Like on a date?" Abby toyed with the simple gold necklace hanging around her neck.

"Yes." He swallowed hard. Damn, when she stated the words so bluntly, he felt nervous. When was the last time he'd had a date? He couldn't remember. The women in his past were a total blur. "I'll pick you up at seven."

"But you don't have a car," she protested.

"Seven," he repeated. "Don't worry about me, just be ready to go by seven."

"All right." Abby stood, a hesitant smile tugging at her mouth. "I guess I'll see you later, then."

He nodded then forced himself to leave. But as he walked back to his motel room across the street, the swell of anticipation made his heart race. He placed a hand over the center of his chest and pressed hard. *Cool it, Tremayne. You're treating Abby to a nice dinner because she deserves it. Keep things light and friendly and you'll do fine.*

In his room, the bed seemed to laugh at him mockingly. He turned his back on it. Kidnapping her and dragging her back to his room was not an option.

Abby had the whole house to herself and she did a little dance as she headed up the stairs. Because she was supposed to be off, her sister Alaina had invited her parents over to her house. Adam was on call. Alec was doing some sort of special SWAT team training. Thank heavens none of her annoying siblings were around to ply her with questions about her plans for the evening.

At times like this, she really, really missed her apartment. Even with Alec living one floor above her. Still, she supposed helping out her parents wasn't the end of the world. Only a few more weeks until she was out on her own again.

Far, far away in another state. Where no one could drop in at a moment's notice to spy on her or make her feel stupid and inept.

She headed into the shower, intent on rinsing thoughts of her family from her mind. Unbelievable how Nick had actually asked her out on a real date. As she scrubbed shampoo through her hair, she couldn't prevent the thrill that played laser-tag along her nerves. The sane, rational part of her brain wondered if this was just another of his pull-me, push-me moves. One minute he'd kissed her, the next he'd shoved her away. Now he'd asked her out. Because he knew she planned to move? Maybe Nick figured she wouldn't ask for more than he could give.

The idea made her pause. Was that true? What did she want from Nick? A brief fling? Her stomach did a back-flip. She wasn't sure she could handle a brief fling with Nick. Too bad she hadn't met him before she'd made arrangements to move. Her feelings toward him were a tangled mess. Yet wasn't she looking for adventure? For too long now the men she was interested in, like Shane, had persisted in seeing her as the girl next door. Aaron's cute little sister. Adam's cute little sister. Or Alec's cute little sister. Or…

But not Nick. When he looked at her through those intense tiger-eyes of his, she didn't feel like the wholesome girl next door at all. Her pulse spiked and she twisted the shower knob toward cold.

When the icy water made her shiver, she turned it off and stepped out. After drying off, she lathered vanillascented lotion over her damp skin. Wrapped in a fluffy towel, she hurried into her room and contemplated the items in her closet. She wanted to wear something flirty and feminine. Alluring.

Sexy.

A flowered sea-green skirt caught her eye, along with a spaghetti-strapped camisole top. Clutching the clothes with one hand, she dug through her dresser drawer with the other until she found the skimpiest pair of panties she owned. The camisole top had a built-in shelf bra, so she donned the flowered outfit and regarded herself critically in the mirror.

Her skirt flared when she gave a quick spin, showing off her tanned legs, one of her best features, if she did say so herself. A wicked grin tugged at her lips. A fling was sounding better and better.

Nick wasn't going to know what hit him.

Abby emerged from the bathroom when she heard the doorbell peal. Thank heavens she was ready. She didn't use much make-up, just a bit to heighten her eyes, and a touch of lipstick was more than enough. But she'd taken a little extra time with her hair, pulling the blond curly mass up on top of her head and leaving just a few tendrils down to frame her face.

She smoothed a hand over her skirt, then headed downstairs. Nick stood straight and tall on the other side of the screen door. His eyes flared and he smiled with appreciation when he saw her. "Hello, Abby. You look lovely."

"Thanks." She cursed herself for sounding breathless when he opened the door. "I'm ready if you are." Rather than inviting him in, she stepped out onto the wide, wraparound porch, invading his space.

"You smell great, too." He lightly clasped her arm, then turned to maneuver the porch steps with his awkward gait. "We have reservations for seven-thirty. I hope you're hungry."

She was ravenous, but not for food. Still, she nodded. "I'm impressed you rented a car just for this."

"You're worth it." His simple statement shot through her heart like an arrow, stealing her breath. "And, in case you're wondering, I haven't taken any meds for over four hours. I'm fine to drive."

She frowned a little, not liking the thought of him being in pain. "Are you sure that's a good idea? I mean about the pain meds, that is. I can drive."

"I'm backing off on the meds anyway, remember?" he answered lightly, but the slanted expression in his eyes warned her to leave it alone.

She settled in the front seat and waited for him to go around to join her. "So, do you know any more about Mr Fischer?" Abby had been concerned the elderly patient was going to end up dying, just like Mr Goetz had. "Did you hear how he's doing?"

Nick reached over the gearshift in the center console to cover her hand with his. "I called the hospital for a status report just before I left. He seems to be doing fine. They have him on a heparin drip and his symptoms haven't gotten any worse."

"Good." Abby sighed in relief. "I'm glad."

Within a few minutes Nick had pulled up to the restaurant. At first she was surprised he used the valet parking, then remembered his cane. She was so accustomed to seeing him walk with it now, she didn't even notice.

Their table was tucked in a secluded corner, with a breathtaking view of Lake Michigan. Everything was so perfect, she was tempted to pinch herself to make sure she wasn't dreaming.

"How about some antipasti for starters?" Nick asked, scanning the menu.

"Sounds great." She already knew exactly what she wanted from the menu—reading the description of the grilled swordfish was making her mouth water.

A discreet waiter took their order. Music from the piano bar drifted over. Nick reached across the table to take her hand in his, pinning her with his intense gaze. "Abby, I need to ask you a question."

Her mouth went dry and she nervously licked her lips. This was it, she already knew what he was going to ask. And what her answer would be. Getting through dinner wouldn't be easy with images of the two of them sharing his motel room tumbling through her head. "Yes?"

His lean fingers lightly stroked her hand. She shivered. But then he pulled away, to reach for his water glass. "What action are you going to take against Roland?"

She blinked. "What?"

"I heard the way he spoke to you, Abby." Nick frowned darkly at her across the table. "Surely you're not going to let that slide without taking some sort of formal action against him? I know very well veterans' hospitals have strict rules about professional conduct."

Please, God, don't tell me Nick asked me out just for this, to grill me about Roland. She struggled to remain calm. "I'd rather not think about him, if you don't mind."

Her weak attempt to change the subject didn't work. Nick leaned earnestly toward her. "Abby, I can help, because I overheard the whole thing."

"I don't believe this." She pushed away from the table.

Now he was the one to look at her warily. "What's wrong?"

"What's wrong?" she echoed as she leaped to her feet.

"Do you see this dress, Nick?" She plucked at the silky fabric. "Do you remember asking me out for dinner because I deserved to be pampered after such a stressful day?"

Wordlessly, he nodded.

"Then why are you obsessed with Roland? Are you so blind that you can't see what's sitting right in front of you?"

"Abby." He stood, using the table for leverage instead of his cane. "Calm down. Of course I see you."

"Do you?" She couldn't seem to find her usual calm demeanor, and didn't care if they were attracting attention from the rest of the patrons in the restaurant. "Do you really? Because I have to tell you, Nick, work was not the reason I came here with you tonight." She leaned toward him. "I had something far more intimate in mind."

"I— Uh, wait a minute, where are you going?" Nick gaped at her when she reached for her purse, slung it over her shoulder and stepped around the table.

"I'm leaving." She didn't care if she never ate swordfish again. So much for her idiotic, romantic notions of having a guy actually like her for herself.

"Don't go, please, Abby. You don't know what you're saying." Nick tried to grasp her hand, but she eluded his grip.

Still, she paused and turned back toward him, making sure he saw the blatant intent in her eyes. "Oh, yes, I do. I know exactly what I'm saying."

Nick ran a frustrated hand over his short hair. "You're driving me crazy. I've met your family, Abby. They are very nice people. I'm trying to be a gentleman, to give you the respect you deserve."

"Oh, yeah?" She lowered her voice, but kept her eyes trained on his. "Did you think maybe your respect isn't what I'm after? I'm more interested in your desire."

CHAPTER EIGHT

Words failed him. Nick would swear the floor undu-
lated beneath his feet. With a determined effort, he
managed to keep his balance.

Barely.

He'd been without female companionship for so
long, he couldn't even believe he was here alone with
Abby in the first place. Work was a neutral conversation topic, he'd figured. A way to keep things light,
easy. Obviously, he'd missed the mark, big time. He'd
be a total fool to pass up her blatant offer.

He wasn't a fool.

Except something nebulous held him back.

Fear of hurting her? Or himself?

"Abby, we're both leaving town soon." As if picking
his way through a minefield, he tried to make her understand what he had trouble articulating. "As much as I
want you, a relationship between us won't go anywhere."

"So?" Her glittering blue eyes challenged him and he
was far too aware of the curious glances they'd garnered
from the others in the restaurant.

He couldn't think of a response. Not when all the blood in his head had pooled in his groin. Dammit, he was trying to be the good guy for once. In the past, he'd boasted a revolving condo door when it came to women, never latching onto one for very long. Until the crash had forced him to reevaluate his life. His priorities.

All his efforts to be a gentleman, to refrain from giving in to the temptation to jump Abby's bones, had been in vain. Only Abby would be upset with him for maintaining control.

Women were confusing, contrary creatures.

Their waiter hurried over. "Is something wrong? Have you changed your mind about having dinner?"

Nick held out a hand toward her, palm upward. "Abby? Will you, please, give me a second chance and stay for dinner?"

With obvious reluctance, she nodded and returned to her seat. Nick chuckled when he heard an audible sigh of relief from the waiter.

"Some wine? Champagne perhaps?" he asked.

Nick caught her gaze with his. "Would you like some champagne?"

"Sure." Her tone was casual, but the tense expression in her eyes was anything but.

"Thanks for staying." Nick would have followed her out, but his body would have suffered for it. For the first time in a long time, his stomach was physically hungry. "After losing so much weight in the hospital, I don't like to skip meals."

A tiny frown puckered her brow as she digested his

words. "I wouldn't want to be responsible for making you skip dinner, so you're welcome."

The champagne and antipasti arrived simultaneously in less than sixty seconds. He wanted to laugh at the waiter's attempt to be invisible, but Abby's lips glistening with champagne sent a stab of heat to his gut. Holding his gaze, she licked a stray drop of champagne from the rim of her glass.

Oh, God. She wanted him.

He swallowed a hasty gulp of his own champagne then choked. The alcohol shot straight to his head, short-circuiting his brain and creating a strange buzzing in his ears. What was wrong with him? He wasn't a dumb college kid any more. Abby wasn't the first woman he'd seduced.

He refused to consider she might be the first one who actually mattered.

Dazed, he watched her smear a bit of sweet tomato relish on a cracker then daintily take a bite. She sucked a stray dollop from the tip of her finger. Every movement was steeped in the unspoken promise of what would come later.

One thing he'd say for Carlo's cuisine, he didn't have to remind himself to eat. Sultry tastes exploded on his tongue, from the tangy tomato relish to the sweet asparagus to the rare grilled tuna.

Food had never tasted so good.

After that first heady sip, he steered clear of the champagne. He hadn't lied about not taking any medication but, still, he did not need to mess up his head any worse than it already was.

"Are you ready to go?" Abby asked, one brow raised questioningly.

Surprised, he glanced down at his empty plate, then back up at her. The unspoken invitation shimmered in her eyes. Hell, yes, he was ready to go. He managed to nod.

"Dessert?" The waiter took one look at two of them staring at each other and shook his head with a wry smile. "Never mind, I'll bring the bill."

Nick imagined sparks would fly if he so much as touched her. Abby ignored the blatant risk of fire and took his hand as they headed outside.

The ride back to his motel room at the Cozy Inn was deafeningly quiet. He silently cursed his cane as he walked alongside Abby. Inside, there was only one low light in the far corner of the room. But other than the little bit of mood lighting, the sterile motel room lacked ambiance. In fact, bringing Abby here suddenly bothered him.

She deserved better than a cheap, hasty coupling in a stark, impersonal motel room.

Hell, she deserved someone better than him. A whole man, willing to do anything for her.

"Abby, wait." He tried to calm his racing heart. To put a little distance between them. Clear his head before he did something he'd regret. "Maybe we should reconsider—"

"What's the matter?" she challenged as she stepped closer and reached out to place her hand on his chest. "Cold feet, Nick?"

"No, they're not cold. They're hot. Really hot." He could feel his slight flash of conscience melting into oblivion. Closing his arms around her, he tugged her close, pressing her softness against his hard length. "But not as hot as you." He reached up to brush his thumbs across her ivory cheeks. "I've never met anyone as beautiful." He wasn't handing her a line, but worried she would take it as one. Why couldn't he find the words to show how much she mattered?

"Then maybe you should kiss me," Abby whispered.

He didn't wait for her to ask twice. He captured her mouth, losing himself in her taste. As much as he wanted to rip her clothes off and tumble her to the bed, he held himself in check. There was no rush.

They had all night.

She tugged at his shirt, trying to free it from his slacks. He was busy doing a little exploring of his own, sliding his hand beneath her skirt, caressing the silky skin of her thigh, and higher still, until he cupped her bottom.

She gave a sexy little moan, rubbing against him. He wanted to see her, every glorious naked inch of her.

"Nick." She plucked at the buttons of his shirt, reading his mind. He didn't want to let her go long enough to help and she finally released the stupid buttons. She didn't waste any time in shoving the cotton fabric off his shoulders.

The sound of her harsh gasp caught him unawares. It took several seconds for the impact to sink in.

His scars.

Dammit, he should have prepared her. His heart twisted when Abby stared at the numerous scars on his chest and shoulder.

The horror reflected in her eyes doused his libido quicker than a swift knee to the groin. He wrenched away.

"No, don't. I'm sorry, I just didn't expect…" She hung onto his arm, attempting to pull him back into her embrace even as she leaned down to press her mouth along the puckered ridge of one jagged scar.

Nick closed his eyes, desperately wishing things were different. Damn. He really was a fool. How could he actually make love to Abby without telling her the truth about Shane? He couldn't. Thank heavens things hadn't gone too far. He could still repair the damage.

He found his voice. "Wait, I need to explain about the scars."

"I'm sorry I reacted so strongly." Abby's self-deprecating gaze tortured him. "I'm a nurse, I know better than to react like that to a few simple scars. I'm sorry. I forgot about your injuries."

He should be glad she'd forgotten about his injuries. He wished he could forget, too. Only guilt wouldn't let him.

"Nick?" She tipped her head to the side. "You and Shane were in the same plane crash, weren't you?"

"Yeah." Admitting the truth helped ease the burden of guilt sitting on his shoulders like a boulder. "We were both in the plane when it crashed. Only I lived and he died."

"I guess I didn't ask because I didn't really want to think about it." Abby stumbled back a step, rubbing her hands along her arms. "I didn't want to imagine the details of how Shane died."

Nick stood in the center of the room, the white scars horribly stark against his skin. His face blanched and he looked as if he wanted to be anywhere else but here. With her.

She took a deep, cleansing breath. From the moment

she'd met Nick, Shane had become the least of her concerns. The deep scars Nick carried had caught her off guard. Seeing the extent of his wounds, the trauma Nick had lived through, was far more upsetting than she'd expected. And right now those were the only details she cared about, the ones affecting Nick.

"What happened?" With a hand on his arm, she urged him to sit on the edge of the bed, then sank to her knees beside him. She sensed he needed to tell the story. She held onto him, wanting the small physical contact to reassure her he was really all right.

"It was my fault. My idea." His movements stiff, he bent down and picked up his shirt from where she'd tossed it on the floor then eased onto one corner of the bed. He stared at the shirt in his hands as if he couldn't bear to meet her gaze. "I convinced Shane we needed to hire a small private plane in order to really appreciate the whole, winding view of the Great Wall of China." He carefully pulled his shirt back on, favoring his injured arm. "Of course, the fact that we couldn't speak a word of Chinese didn't seem to matter. Heck, why would I be concerned with actually communicating with the pilot of our plane?"

His sarcasm flayed her already aching heart. "Nick, I knew Shane, remember? Trust me. You didn't make him do anything he didn't want to do."

Nick continued as if he hadn't heard her. "We weren't in the air more than fifteen or twenty minutes when I noticed we were losing altitude. Then suddenly we were heading straight toward a huge ridge of trees. I screamed at the pilot to pull up the nose and hit the throttle, but he didn't speak English any better than we spoke Chinese. We skimmed along the tops of the trees and for a minute I thought we were going to make it out of there. But then something caught on the wing and we slammed into a tree, nose first. The plane lodged in the branches. My side of the craft took the brunt of the damage."

Abby swallowed the lump in her throat. She could envision the crash so clearly.

"We guessed the pilot died on impact. Or maybe even went unconscious before when the plane lost control—who knows? Shane was able to climb out of the wreck but…I couldn't. I was pinned between the plane and the tree." He scrubbed his hands over his face. "He wanted to stay with me but his cell phone wouldn't pick up a signal. I wanted him to walk away from the wreck until he could call for help. But he wouldn't listen."

He paused and she held her breath, waiting for him to finish the story.

"He stayed with me and while he struggled to pull at the part of the plane where I was trapped, the engine broke free and fell on top of him, dragging him out of the tree."

"Oh, Nick." She reached up, intent on giving him a hug, but he remained stiff and unyielding.

"I could see him lying on the ground beneath me." Nick was staring out into space, reliving the horror. "I called out to him the whole time I struggled to get out. No matter how hard I shoved against the crushed metal, I couldn't seem to budge. I'm not sure how long I worked at it, but eventually I found a way to escape the wreckage."

He turned his head to meet her gaze. "I fell to the

ground and crawled to Shane, but I was too late. He was already dead."

She felt bad for Shane but felt even worse for Nick. He'd suffered far more. Praying she sounded calmer than she felt, she asked, "How on earth did you manage to get rescued?"

"Shane's cell phone. I managed to make my way to a clearing and found a signal." He glanced away and she could only imagine how he must have crawled on his belly to find the clearing. "If I had worked harder to convince him to leave, to get away from the damn plane, he'd be alive today."

"And if the situation were reversed, if Shane had been pinned in the wreck, would you have left him?" She reached up and smoothed a hand over his chest. "I don't think so."

"Maybe." But the doubt in his tone belied his words. "Either way, it was still my stupid idea. I chartered the damn plane. Hired the idiot who couldn't fly."

"And I bet the view of the wall was breathtaking."

"Maybe, but it sure as hell wasn't worth Shane's life." Nick brushed her hand from his chest, as if her touch seared him. "So now you know the truth. I should have told you right from the very beginning."

"It doesn't matter, Nick."

He ignored her. "I was airlifted to a hospital in the States. A box of my belongings was shipped back, but I found lots of Shane's stuff with mine. That's how I ended up with your letters. I made it my mission to bring them back to you."

"I understand." And now her outrage at how he'd read

them seemed petty. Nick had nearly died. Her mind couldn't seem to wrap itself around that gigantic fact. "I don't mind."

He gave her a strange look. "I need to take you home."

Leaving Nick like this was the last thing Abby wanted to do. But she could see the stubborn glint to his eyes, the same one he'd worn the first night she'd met him. Nothing short of a rocket blaster would get him to change his mind.

"You could walk me home instead," she offered. "After that wonderful meal, a little exercise would be good."

"Sure." He avoided her gaze and headed for the door.

Following him out was more difficult than she'd imagined. If only she could go back, to the moment she'd overreacted to his scars, she'd do things so differently.

During the walk to her parents' house, a thick silence hung between them. She racked her brain for a way to bring back the earlier tone of the evening.

But she suspected it was gone for good.

She stopped on the sidewalk in front of her parents' house. "Thanks for dinner, Nick. I had a wonderful time."

He stared at her for a moment, his gaze shadowed by the dim light of the streetlamp, then shook his head with exasperation. "Why aren't you angry or upset with me? I know how much you cared about Shane. Your letters revealed the depth of your feelings."

Abby supposed she should be embarrassed at how Nick had glimpsed into her heart, but she couldn't summon up the emotion. Instead, she tipped her head to the side. "You're right about how much I cared for Shane, but do you honestly think I place a higher value on Shane's life than I do yours?"

"You should. He was a good man. Loyal to a fault." He arched a brow. "He cared enough about you to save your letters."

"I know." She couldn't help but smile. Knowing Shane had saved her letters helped ease the pain of losing him, at least a little. "He was a great guy, but we can't go back and change the past. Things happen for a reason, Nick."

He hesitated. "You really believe that?"

"I do." Her voice echoed with conviction.

"I wish I could say the same." Nick toyed with a strand of her hair. "All those months in the hospital, unable to feed myself or get to the bathroom under my own power, I kept wondering, Why me? Why did Shane die instead of me?"

She didn't know how to respond to that. "And now that you're out and healing?"

He shook his head and dropped his hand to his side. "I may be out of the hospital, but I'm far from being healed. I may never be able to return to the OR. And if that's true, I have no clue what the hell I'm going to do with the rest of my life."

Abby caught his hand as he turned away. She couldn't let him leave like this. "Nick, wait." She tugged him close and leaned up to kiss him.

He turned so that her kiss missed its mark, barely brushing his cheek. "No, I have to go. Goodbye, Abby."

Helpless, she could only watch him leave.

CHAPTER NINE

ABBY walked to work, hoping the fresh air would combat her exhaustion. Last night, Nick's rejection had hurt more than she'd thought possible. She hadn't been able to sleep because their dinner had been so fun, so full of anticipation, until her stupidity had ruined everything.

And they hadn't been able to go back to the way things had been. No matter how much she longed to.

When she had finally fallen asleep, her dreams had been just as exhausting as her day had been. She'd dreamed she had been at work where Shane and Nick were both patients of hers and she'd run from one to the other, trying to help them both but succeeding in helping neither.

The quietness of the morning was a blessing. Taking a deep breath helped clear the sleepy fog from her mind. The summer day was a perfect seventy degrees. Too bad she had to go into work. Would she see Nick today? Yesterday had been one of her scheduled days off, but after today she had the whole weekend to herself.

Maybe she could convince Nick to spend the time with her.

If he wasn't back in avoidance mode.

When she walked onto the rehab floor, there was no sign of him. Ridiculous to be disappointed, it was still pretty early. She shouldn't be surprised. Most of the physicians didn't show up until well after eight for rounds.

Except for Roland, who didn't show up much at all.

"Hi, Abby," Irene greeted her. "We're short-handed, down one because Rachel called in sick again today."

She stifled a groan. "All right, it's nothing we haven't worked through before. Did we at least get a third nursing assistant?"

"Yes, thank heavens."

"OK, we'll have to pretty much take seven patients apiece, and each nurse will have their own nurse's aide to help." Abby stared at the census board, trying to figure out the fairest way to split up the patient assignments.

Finally, they divvied up the patients and listened to report. Abby started her day making rounds of the newer patients she didn't know very well. She took her time assessing them so she wouldn't miss anything. Mr Fischer's stroke symptoms remained far too fresh in her memory.

By midmorning she was starting to feel pretty good about staying caught up with her work.

"Abby?"

She spun round when Irene called her name.

"Your patient, Mr Cooper, is down in PT, requesting additional pain medication. The therapist just called up here asking if you'd run some down."

Abby nodded. "I know Mr Cooper has had a few rough days lately. Will you keep an eye on my patients for me?"

"No problem."

Abby remembered the last time she'd gone down to the gym, when poor Mr Goetz had suffered his seizure. As she took the stairs, she wondered if Roland even realized Mr Goetz had died. Or if he cared.

She found Mr Cooper using the parallel bars, trying to walk with his new prosthesis. He'd lost one leg due to problems with circulation and he often complained of phantom pain in that leg. Once he'd mastered walking with the new prosthesis, he'd be able to return home.

"Hi, Mr Cooper. Here's the pain medication you requested." The physical therapist stood nearby, watching to make sure Mr Cooper didn't fall. "I'll get you a cup of water, then let you get back to work."

She turned and caught sight of Nick, lifting weights with his injured leg on the equipment on the opposite side of the room. His gray T-shirt was damp with sweat, clinging to his chest and biceps as he fought against resistance of the weights. Another physical therapist hovered nearby, keeping an eye on Nick.

After finishing with Mr Cooper, she smiled and approached Nick. He stared at a spot on the wall behind her and made deep, grunting noises as he lifted his leg up then down.

"Hello," she greeted him. "Are you heading up to the unit later?"

Nick didn't smile, barely looked at her to even acknowledge she was standing there. With a slight nod he continued to remain totally focused while he exercised his muscles like a madman.

She wasn't sure if he'd actually responded to her question or had simply acknowledged her presence, but clearly he was far too preoccupied to talk. Swallowing a stupid flare of pique, she spun away, leaving Nick to face his demons alone.

Upstairs, Irene was having a tough time getting one of her patients transferred to a nursing home. For the next couple of hours Abby was too busy to agonize over Nick.

Abby finally sat down at the computer to complete her documentation when she heard a loud thunk.

"What was that?" She jumped back to her feet and hurried to the room directly across from the nurses' station, where the emergency light was flashing.

Blood splatters stained the walls, the sheets of the bed, the linoleum and the patient lying on his side on the floor near the foot of the bed. The bed alarm shrilled loudly and she snapped it off then fell to her knees beside the patient, her heart in her throat. "Mr Krantz! What happened?"

"Ooh," he groaned, and rolled onto his back. Dark brown stains smeared his sweatpants.

"Oh, no, you had diarrhea again, didn't you? You poor thing." Mr Krantz wasn't normally her patient, but she knew he continued to be plagued by these episodes where he needed to get to a bathroom in a hurry. But the diarrhea didn't explain where all the blood had come from.

"Stay still, don't move." She placed a hand on his arm to hold him steady. "Wendy?" She raised her voice, calling for the nursing assistant. "Have Irene call Dr Roland, stat. Mr Krantz fell and hit his head."

The cut on his forehead had bled, but not much. She moved down to the red spot on his gown and found it. Somehow he must have gotten his hand tangled in his central line and had pulled it out.

She glanced back over her shoulder. Sure enough, he'd been hooked up to the IV pump to get his IV anti-biotics, too. Except the tail end of the IV catheter was still in his bed, where the linen had soaked up the medication.

"Wiggle your fingers and toes for me." She was afraid to move him too much in case he'd fractured his hip or his spine. Leaving him on the floor bothered her, and she threw an impatient glance toward the doorway. What the heck was taking Irene and Wendy so long? "Tell me what hurts."

"My hip. I landed on it funny." The older gentleman's eyes were full of apology. "I know I was supposed to call first, but I didn't think there would be enough time…"

"Shh, it's OK. Don't worry, we'll get you cleaned up and up off the floor in a jiffy," Abby hastened to reassure him. Wendy and Irene rushed in, carrying a long white backboard.

Between the three of them, they carefully log-rolled Mr Krantz onto the backboard and then lifted him onto the bed. Abby sent Wendy for a fresh patient gown and sheets so they could get the worst of the blood and diarrhea cleaned up.

"What happened?" Nick's deep voice made Abby glance up in surprise. What was he doing here? After his mute act in the physical therapy gym, she'd figured he had the day off. But here he was, freshly showered, a nice shirt and slacks replacing his sweaty clothes.

"Mr Krantz tried to get up by himself to go to the bathroom while he was getting his IV antibiotics. He fell, hit his head on the floor, may have fractured his hip, and pulled out his central line."

Nick's brows drew together in a concerned frown. "Where does he hurt the most?"

"His hip. But I think he'll need his entire body X-rayed just to be sure. Do you think we should call someone to replace his central line before he goes to Radiology or after?"

"Before, in case they need venous access down there to give him contrast. I'll order a CT scan of his head, too, just to be sure."

Abby wasn't about to argue. "I'll call the radiology procedure area to see if they have an empty room and someone available to place the line."

"I can replace the line, so just worry about a bed." Nick sounded confident.

She wanted to ask if actually putting in a central line was part of a consultant's duties but decided the issue wasn't her problem. Mr Krantz needed care, and if Nick was willing to place the line for him, she wouldn't complain. Besides, she'd paged Roland and he still hadn't responded.

"Can you help me transport the patient down to the procedure area?" Nick wanted to know.

It was on the tip of her tongue to refuse. She had other things to do, like start the mountain of documentation that a patient fall required, but then she caught sight of Mr Krantz's worried gaze. Her impatience melted.

"Sure." She could probably get on a computer down in

Radiology and if not, she'd do the work on her own time. She couldn't let Mr Krantz go down alone. "I'll help."

Downstairs, the procedure area was extremely busy. There was only one empty bed and they rolled Mr Krantz into the slot. While Nick went to work, preparing the patient for the new central line, she quickly accessed the nearby computer workstation to begin her documentation.

But after about ten minutes Nick muttered something under his breath and pushed the procedure table aside with his foot.

"Mr Krantz, I'm going to need someone to assist in getting this line in. I'll be right back. Are you doing all right?"

"Yeah. Fine." Mr Krantz's voice was faint.

Abby quickly logged off the computer and went to his side. "I'm here, Mr Krantz."

"My hip hurts."

She met Nick's gaze. "How about giving him some pain medication?"

"Sure. Does he have any ordered?"

"Yes, actually, he does." Abby had just accessed his record, and the percocet order was still valid.

"Give him whatever he already has ordered."

Abby called the pharmacy to request the dose. Nick disappeared, then returned a few minutes later with another doctor.

The second physician placed the central line in about fifteen minutes. The percocets she'd requested arrived as soon as they finished.

Instead of taking Mr Krantz upstairs to his room, Nick

arranged for him to have all his X-rays taken. In the fifteen minutes that had passed since he'd gotten his pain medication, Mr Krantz had relaxed, dozing on his cart.

"We'll take him from here," the radiology tech informed them with a cheerful smile.

Abby let Mr Krantz go, then walked with Nick to the elevators. The closed expression on Nick's face told her he was still upset at not being able to place the line. "He must be a difficult patient to find access on."

"No, he's not." Nick jabbed the elevator button. "Didn't you notice how easy it was for Dr Jericho to insert the line?"

She shrugged, not completely understanding what his problem was. "Sometimes new catheters go in easy, and sometimes they don't."

They stepped into the elevator and the doors closed. "The problem wasn't with Mr Krantz. The problem was with me." Nick opened and closed his hand. "My finger dexterity wasn't good enough to place one measly central line. I couldn't cannulate the subclavian vein. Guess that's proof that returning to surgery is out." His expression turned grim. "For good."

Abby didn't know what to say. She couldn't imagine what she'd do if someone told her she couldn't be a nurse any more.

But, then again, Nick was still a doctor. Just because he couldn't do surgery, it didn't mean there was no hope of a medical career.

"Can you treat trauma patients from a medical perspective yet stay out of surgery?" she asked, as they returned to the rehab floor.

"No." Nick's denial was instant.

She tried again. "I can imagine trauma is thrilling, but isn't there a lot of death, too?"

"Sometimes. But there's nothing like the adrenaline rush of knowing there's an unstable trauma on its way in. There's a challenge in taking someone extremely broken and putting them back together again."

"Maybe, but do you want to know what I like about rehab?"

Nick didn't answer, so she hurried on. "The patients have gotten through the worst of their traumatic injury and now they're on the way home. For the most part, they communicate with me. They're anxious to learn how to take care of themselves, eager to be independent. The care here is positive, building strength both physically and mentally." She wished she could make him understand. "I like the fact that my patients rarely die. I like knowing they're on the final leg of their medical journey, ready to make new adjustments for the reward of going home."

He narrowed his gaze. "Obviously you love your job as much as I did."

She squared her jaw. He wasn't the only one who could be stubborn. "Yes, I do. But your career isn't over, Nick. Maybe you can't operate any more, but there is so much you can do. Look at all the wonderful things you've done as a consultant up here. I think the reason you're so good at this is because you understand, more than anyone, the impact of traumatic injuries."

He was silent for so long she thought he was simply ignoring her, but then he finally spoke. "So basically you think physical medicine is the perfect choice for a cripple like me? Sorry, but, no, thanks. I'm a surgeon and I'm not ready to give up. This conversation is over. I'm out of here."

She couldn't think of a way to stop him from walking away. Nick wasn't just running from her, he was running from himself.

And she didn't know how to help him face the truth.

Nick managed to avoid Abby for the most part during the next few days. She'd had a few shifts off and even on the days she was working, he didn't stop to chat but concentrated on finishing his rounds.

Over the past week and a half, he had noticed Roland slacking off on his rounds. He'd set up a meeting with Johnson the day before to discuss his concerns and was satisfied that the chief of staff would be issuing Roland with a warning—either see his patients on a regular basis or risk having his admitting privileges revoked.

Nick hadn't seen Abby since that morning. Now, since the hour was close to four, he assumed she'd already gone home. He should have been relieved, but part of him had wanted to see her once more.

He made his way downstairs, leaving the rehab unit. Last night he'd decided his temporary job here was finished. He'd packed his duffel bag earlier that morning and requested a late check-out from his room at the Cozy Inn. The only thing he had left to do was to get in touch with Johnson personally to let him know, with apologies for the short notice, that he was leaving.

Not just the hospital, but Milwaukee. He'd booked a nine o'clock flight. Without a real place to call home, Nick figured he'd return to Virginia, and to the hospital where he'd worked before leaving for Beijing.

He'd finish his physical therapy, and then what? He had no idea. If he couldn't be a surgeon, he wasn't sure what he'd do.

For a moment, he toyed with the idea of calling Abby to tell her he was leaving, but resisted the urge. She had the power to make him forget his plan, to turn him inside out. The last time he'd seen her, he'd almost taken things too far. He knew if she asked him to stay longer, he just might be tempted.

Even though he had nothing to offer her.

He thought for a moment about Shane. If he had lived, Shane would have asked Abby out. They would have developed a relationship.

What did he know about relationships? Nothing. And he needed to figure out his own life before inflicting himself on a woman.

Nick walked outside, squinting in the bright sunlight. He began to cross the back employee parking lot when he heard raised, heated voices.

"Do you have any idea what you've done to me, you little bitch?"

"I didn't do anything to you, Dr Roland. You did this completely on your own." Abby's voice, steady and firm, reached his ears.

"You tried to ruin my career."

"Stop it! Let me go!"

Nick's eyes finally adjusted to the bright sunlight and

for an awful moment he had a clear picture of Abby struggling with Roland near a fancy, royal blue convertible.

He quickened his pace, but before he'd closed the
distance between them he saw Roland tighten his grip
on Abby's shoulders and shake her, hard.

She cried out in alarm, shoving against his chest.
"Stop it! You're hurting me."

"Let her go!" Nick shouted. Roland glanced his way
and Abby took advantage of the moment, grinding one
heel against his instep and at the same time yanking free
from his bruising grip.

"Dammit." Roland scowled when Abby broke free.
He lunged for her, but she anticipated his move and
sidestepped him. His fist latched onto her scrubs just
enough to give him a good grip, and he yanked her
toward him with surprising force.

This time Abby fought with a sense of wild desper-
ation. Nick willed his injured muscles to move faster,
but the scene continued to unfold before him in slow
motion.

"Let me go!" Abby's face grew red as she struggled
against Roland's grip. Knocked off balance, they both fell
against the car, with Abby pinned beneath Roland's bulk.

Nick grabbed the back of Roland's shirt and hauled
him upright, away from Abby. "Stop it! What is your
problem?"

Nick smelled the odor of alcohol and he knew.

Drunk. Roland was drunk. Maybe not staggering,
stupid drunk, but definitely under the influence.

Roland ignored Nick, his attention still focused on
Abby, and he glared at her where she leaned against the

car. "What do you have against me, huh? What did I ever do to you?"

"You've crossed the line, Roland." Nick was hesitant to let go of him, worried that he'd lunge for Abby again. "Stay away from her, do you hear me?"

"It's all her fault. Everything is all her fault." Roland continued to babble, but Nick sensed the worst of the danger was over. "She's trying to ruin me."

He shoved Roland aside with disgust then crossed over to Abby and drew her upright, pressing her against his lean frame. The dazed, horrified expression in her eyes tore at him. "Are you all right?"

"Yes." Her hands were shaking, and she reached down to massage her knee. She must have smacked it hard on the car when they'd fallen against it.

Nick barely glanced at Roland, but dug his cell phone out of his lab coat and punched in 911. "You'd better file formal assault charges this time, Abby. If you don't, I will."

CHAPTER TEN

"Don't be ridiculous." Abby straightened then snatched the phone from his hand. "You can't call 911 for this. It's not an emergency."

"You're hurt. That's enough of an emergency for me." Furious at Roland for laying a hand on Abby, he rounded on him, wrapping a fist in the front of his shirt. "You better stay away from her."

"Nick." Abby laid a hand on his arm. "I'm fine. Just let it go."

"I can't." Those endless moments before he could reach her would haunt him. "He threatened you."

"Threatened her? Hell, I just wanted to talk to her." Roland leaned backward, trying to break Nick's hold. Apparently Roland wasn't willing to pick on someone his own size. "I didn't mean to hurt her."

"Oh, yeah? Maybe you should have thought of that before you grabbed her and shook her like a rag doll." Abby continued to pull on Nick's arm, and with reluctance he let go of Roland's shirt. Taking a step back, he breathed deeply, struggling for control. "Get the hell out of here, Roland. And don't even think about getting behind the wheel in your condition because I'll call the police. Did I mention Abby's brother is a cop?" He took his cell phone back from Abby. "Go inside and call yourself a cab."

Roland stumbled away, muttering under his breath. Letting him walk off wasn't easy—adrenaline sped through Nick's system, making him yearn to blow off some steam by following Roland inside. He wrestled himself under control and turned toward Abby. "Let me see your knee."

She lifted one leg of her scrub pants as high as it would go. Her right knee was swollen and already starting to bruise.

"We need to get some ice. I'll run inside the hospital for some."

"No." Abby's voice was flat. "Roland's in there."

He understood her reluctance and glanced across the street to the Cozy Inn, where he had a room—at least until five o'clock. "We can get ice from the motel. Do you think you can make it that far?"

"Sure." She sounded confident enough but when she put her weight on her knee, she winced. "Maybe."

"Here, you lean on me, I'll lean on my cane," he joked, trying not to sound as frustrated as he felt. Why couldn't he have moved just a little faster, to prevent Roland from hurting her?

Why hadn't his muscles obeyed his commands? If he hadn't been hampered by his injuries, he could have stopped Roland and defused the situation before things had got out of hand.

"Stop it." Abby must have been able to read his mind, because she jabbed him once in the ribs. "You've got to stop taking responsibility for other people's actions. Roland's antics hurt my knee—you didn't. Besides, I was stupid enough to try talking to him in the first place."

Nick raised a brow as they made their way across the street. "Did you smell the alcohol on his breath?"

She sighed. "Not until after I was too close. Then, when I tried to back off, he grabbed me. He was so angry, nothing I said got through to him."

He wondered if her wrist was bruised as well and vowed to take a closer look once they were inside. They crossed the mostly vacant parking lot of the motel. Inside the building, he hesitated outside the door to his room. The packed duffel was standing just inside the door. Well, there wasn't anything he could do about it now. With a sinking feeling in the pit of his stomach, he opened the door and helped her in.

The muscles in her body stiffened the moment she caught sight of his bag.

"You're leaving?"

"Yeah."

"Tonight?"

He nodded.

"Without saying goodbye?" Her tone was incredulous.

Nick concentrated on getting Abby over to the bed, where she could sit and take the pressure off her knee. This was exactly what he'd tried to avoid. The wounded expression in her eyes sliced him like a scalpel.

"Sit down, I'll get you some ice." Once she was

settled on the edge of the bed, he grabbed the ice bucket and a plastic bag, then headed out to the ice machine at the end of the hall. Filling the ice bucket halfway only took a minute, and when he returned to his room, the wounded look in her eyes was still there.

Awkwardly, he knelt before her and gently pressed the makeshift cold pack on the swollen part of her knee. Because she kept staring at him, he felt compelled to respond.

"Abby, not long ago I discovered you were moving to Florida and today you're upset because I was going to leave without saying goodbye?" He trailed a finger down her ivory cheek, noting how her freckles stood out in sharp contrast to her skin. "We don't want the same things, Abby. I never intended to hurt you." Damn, now he sounded just like Roland.

"So where are you going?" She stared at his duffel, placed neatly against the wall by the door. Slowly she brought her gaze to his. "I mean, I know you're going home, but where is home? In Chicago?"

Chicago? Where had she got that idea? Then he remembered telling her he'd grown up there, that they were practically neighbors. There wasn't any specific place he'd ever thought of as home. It was on the tip of his tongue to admit the truth, but he caught himself just in time. "Not Chicago. I have a condo across from the Fairfax Hospital in Virginia."

"Oh. I see. It sounds nice."

Nice? His condo wasn't nice. It was empty. Lonely. And about as impersonal as this motel room. He'd bought it furnished a year or so ago, and would have been ashamed to show Abby the place. He didn't have any personal belongings there. No books, no art, no family pictures.

Besides of his clothes, there was nothing in the place except what he'd bought originally.

His so-called home was as far from the noisy, crowded Monroe household, with its comfortable, eclectic furniture and wall of framed photographs, as you could get.

Before he could gather his thoughts, she shoved at his hand holding the ice on her knee. "It's too cold," she protested. "I'm fine."

Dark smudges encircling her wrist caught his gaze, and he set the ice aside and took her hand in his. "Look what that bastard did to you."

"I'm fine," she repeated in a stubborn tone, but he didn't believe her. The fine tremor in her hands ripped at him. Dammit, what would Roland have done if he hadn't gotten there in time?

"Shh." He bent and placed a quick kiss on the bruises marring her wrist. "It's OK. I'm here for you."

"For a minute, when I was pinned underneath him, I couldn't breathe…" She didn't finish.

"I know." Nick tightened his grip and smoothed a hand over her hair. "I'm sorry I didn't get to you sooner."

She shook her head. Her lack of feistiness bothered him more than he wanted to admit. He stood, ignoring the pain in his leg, then settled beside her on the edge of the bed. The mattress dipped, bringing her body closer to his. He wrapped his arm around her shoulders and held her against him.

To his surprise, she slid one arm around his waist and turned into his embrace, tucking her head into the curve of his shoulder.

He wanted to erase the awful memories from her mind. Seated as they were, side by side on the bed, he couldn't hold her as close as he wanted. With a quick motion he lifted her knees and turned her so she was sitting on his lap.

Tense, he waited for her to break out of his arms, but she didn't. Instead, Abby held on tight.

He didn't know how long he held her, only that he withstood the pain in his leg for as long as possible, before shifting her weight to the other side.

She uttered a soft moan, but didn't stir.

He realized she must have fallen asleep.

Careful not to wake her, he slid backwards until they were both stretched out on the bed. He drew one end of the bedspread over her, then tucked her against his chest. With his chin nestled in her hair, he relaxed against the pillow.

If all he could do for Abby was to give her an hour of peaceful sleep, that's what he'd do.

Although holding her in his arms like this, before he was scheduled to leave, was sweet torture.

A fierce banging woke Abby from a sound sleep. Confused, she lifted her head and glanced around.

"Open up, Tremayne! I know you're in there." The words were emphasized by more pounding.

"Stop it, I'm coming." Abby crawled from the bed, straightening her scrubs as she did. Nick stirred on the bed. The room was dark, she and Nick must have slept for hours.

"Abby? Dammit, open this door or I'll break it in!"

Knowing her brother wasn't kidding, she flicked on the light and wrenched the door open. "Alec, what is your problem?"

"What are you guys doing hanging around here?" Dressed in full cop gear, Alec shouldered past her, scanning the room like a madman. "Do you realize we just busted a drug deal in a room on the second floor of this motel?"

"A drug deal?" Abby stared at him. "What does that have to do with us?" Abby shut the door, trying hard not to slam it. Nick had already risen to his feet and stood on the opposite side of the double bed, watching her brother with a wary eye. "You're acting crazy, busting in here like a madman."

"Why didn't you answer your phone?" Alec didn't give an inch, standing with a wide stance as if he was ready to go for his gun at any second.

With a guilty flush, Abby glanced around for her purse. She'd left it on the floor near the bed. Picking it up, she found the cell phone she'd left on vibrate. There were nine missed calls.

"I was busy." After turning the phone off, she tossed it back on the floor. Heavens, save her from four older, overprotective brothers.

"Too busy to consider Mom?" Alec challenged as his accusing glance swept over the wrinkled bed and to her equally wrinkled clothes.

Guilt burned the back of her throat like lye. "I'm

sorry. Maybe I should have called, but I'm not the only child she has. And that's no excuse for your behavior, Alec. You're wired just a little too tight."

Nick found his voice. "But now that he's here, tell him what happened with Roland. I know you were more upset than you let on."

Alec's gaze narrowed, bounced between the two of them. "What do you mean? What happened?"

Great, just what she needed—more fuel to pour on her brother's fiery temper. She shot Nick a look, warning him to shut up. "Nothing. Never mind."

"What happened?" Ignoring her, Alec addressed Nick.

"One of the doctors was drunk, grabbed her shoulders and shook her hard enough to make her teeth rattle. Then when she tried to escape, he grabbed her again, then fell on her, pinning her against the car." Nick gestured toward her. "She has the bruises to prove it."

Alec spun toward her.

"Forget it." She crossed her arms and resisted the urge to scream at the top of her lungs. What was it about her brothers that made them deaf and dumb when it came to her wishes? "You come storming in here like some psycho and now you want to talk rationally? Get out, Alec. I'm twenty-six years old. I don't need you to watch over me." A strangled laugh bubbled out. "This is exactly why I can't wait to move to Florida. You know, after this stunt of yours, I might not even bother to give you my address once I'm settled."

Her brother clenched his jaw. "We had a right to be worried. Let me see your bruises. Who is this guy? We can still pick him up for assault."

"You're not arresting anyone." She glanced at her watch. "It's ten o'clock at night. Don't you have real bad guys to catch? Go chase your drug dealers and leave me alone."

Alec stared at her for a long minute, as if reassuring himself she was really all right. Then he moved toward the door. "Mom and Dad were wondering what happened to you. You'd better call them."

"Fine," she snapped. "Now get out."

Alec noticed Nick's bag propped beside the door. He raised a brow at him. "Leaving?"

Nick shrugged. "Eventually. Why?"

"Just wondering." Alec's gaze widened innocently. "See you later, Abby."

"Not if I can help it." Reaching out, she shoved Alec, surprising him enough to make him stumble. Satisfaction surged. "Goodbye, Alec."

When the door closed behind her brother, she dropped onto the edge of the bed and cradled her head in her hands. Her voice was muffled. "I'm sorry."

"Why? Because you have a family who cares about you?" Nick limped over to pick up his cane.

"No, because they're psychotic." With a deep sigh, she lifted her head. "Especially my brothers. Alec is worse, much worse, since he became a cop. You can see why I'm so desperate to get away from them."

"I still think you should have told your brother about Roland," Nick argued. "He deserves to be punished for what he did to you." He stepped around the bed. His leg buckled and he almost fell on the bed, catching himself just in time.

Abby frowned. Had Nick re-injured his leg? He'd continued to work out in the physical therapy gym each morning, on top of his consultancy work. She suspected he'd cut way back on his pain medication, too. The incident with Roland probably hadn't helped either.

She tensed and shivered. Heck, maybe Nick was right. But if she did decide to press charges, her brother would be the last person she'd go to.

"I meant to thank you for coming to my rescue."

"It was pure, dumb luck that I happened to be there."

She didn't agree, more like fate intervening before he could leave without saying goodbye. She shook off the despondent thought. "Do you think Roland has a drinking problem? Maybe his drinking is the reason he hasn't been making rounds?"

"I don't know." Nick pursed his lips. "I guess I thought Johnson had given him an ultimatum and as a result Roland went out and had a few drinks." He raised a brow. "Unless you think he's been under the influence before?"

"Er…no." She wrinkled her brow, thinking back to their extremely brief conversations. "At least, not that I can say for sure. There was one time I thought he slurred his words, but then he seemed fine."

"It's a big leap from one or two episodes of drinking too much to a full-fledged alcohol problem that could interfere with his work."

Abby didn't necessarily agree. "Not really. I mean, honestly, Nick, how would we know? He's hardly ever around to smell the alcohol on him. What do we know about his mental condition while he's giving orders to us from the other end of a phone?"

"You have a point," Nick agreed. He came around the bed, but didn't come close enough to touch her.

She wished, more than anything, she could have woken up in his arms. To have kissed him one last time.

Nick stared at her, a frown furrowing his brow. "I don't know where to go from here."

Abby swallowed hard and tried to sound casual, although her heart was thumping in her chest. "Why? Because you missed your flight?"

"Partially." He shrugged, then turned away. "I guess this means I'm not leaving after all."

"You're not?" Hope swelled at his words. Even after her brother's rudeness, Nick was staying.

Nick was staying.

"No, I think there's something going on with Roland."

Abby wanted to tell him how glad she was that he wasn't leaving yet but didn't want him to take her comment the wrong way. She wasn't trying to plan an entire future with him, but surely they had a relationship of sorts.

"You mean you think he could have a drinking problem?"

Nick nodded. "Yeah. Now that you've put the idea in my head, I can't leave until I know for sure that Roland isn't practicing under the influence of alcohol. Because if he is, he either needs to sign himself into a treatment program or have his license suspended until he agrees to go."

"Sounds like a plan." Abby smoothed a hand over her wrinkled scrubs. She hoped Roland wouldn't be around much longer. And Nick staying would give her time to make a few phone calls. There was no reason she had to go all the way to Florida to get away from her family.

Virginia would work just as well.

CHAPTER ELEVEN

As Nick walked Abby home, the idea of moving to Virginia grew, expanding in her chest. The nursing shortage was prevalent everywhere, there must be traveling nurse assignments in Virginia, too. There were still a couple of weeks before she was scheduled to leave. Easy enough to call the traveling nurse agency and request they switch her assignment. Giddy, she felt as if she were walking on air. The distance between Nick's motel and home was almost too short. They reached her parents' house in record time.

Nick stopped at the foot of the stairs leading to the wide wrap-around porch. "Goodnight, Abby." His hand tightened on hers.

"Goodnight, Nick." When he would have walked away, she leaned up to kiss him. This time he didn't duck fast enough. Her intention had been to keep things light, but in a heartbeat his mouth fused with hers.

He pulled her close, the thin fabric of her scrubs an invisible barrier between their bodies. She reveled in every hard, glorious inch of him.

Then he broke off the kiss, breathing heavily. "The taste of you goes straight to my head, Abby."

It was the nicest thing any man had ever said to her. "And this is a bad thing?" she teased.

"You got it." Nick cleared his throat and took another step back. "I'd better go, before one of your brothers shows up."

Irritation flashed, dark and lethal. "They don't run my life, Nick, no matter what they think. I'm moving out of here as soon as possible."

"Easy, Abby." Nick held up a hand. "I was only joking. I think it's sweet the way they look out for you."

"It's not sweet." Her buoyant mood had been shattered by her family's interference once again. With a sigh she rubbed her forehead. "Never mind. Will I see you tomorrow?"

"Sure. I'll call you." Nick bent to give her one more quick kiss, then turned and headed back down the street the way they'd come.

She wanted very badly to follow him, to go anywhere but inside. The house was quiet, her parents were sleeping peacefully, despite Alec's attempt to make her feel guilty. She couldn't believe Nick hadn't been angry at her brother's irrational behavior. The nerve of him, barging into Nick's motel room to find her, playing on her mother's concern. Which was totally ridiculous. Other than needing a little help moving around, her mother was doing fine.

In fact, her mother was doing so well, there was no reason to wait until the middle of August to leave.

She was going to put in her notice on Monday.

Waiting the entire weekend would be hard, but at least she could spend the time with Nick.

Thinking of all the various ways they might pass the time carried her erotic visions into her dreams.

Nick headed over to the physical therapy gym first thing next morning. The manager of the Cozy Inn had been more than happy for Nick to extend his visit a few more days, especially after the bad press of the drug bust. At least Alec hadn't been lying about that. He'd considered relocating to a different motel, but the manager had given him a discount to stay.

As much as he'd wanted to leave, to get far away from the temptation of Abby, he couldn't go without uncovering the truth about Roland.

Had Abby stumbled on the truth? Did Roland have a drinking problem? He hoped not.

After his physical therapy session, he planned to wander up to the rehab unit. Good thing he'd never gotten in touch with Johnson about leaving, so his position was secure.

Nick strained his muscles to the limit on the weight machines, even though he couldn't help suspecting his efforts were in vain. Pumping all the iron in the world wasn't going to replace the damaged nerves in his hand to the point he could go back to being a surgeon.

Walking without the help of a damn cane was still a good motivator, though, so he concentrated on his working his legs, lifting weights until his muscles screamed and trembled with agony.

After a long, hot shower, Nick put on his lab coat

over his casual clothes and headed up to the rehab unit. When he walked on the floor, the first thing he saw was a brand-new patient lying in the hallway, waiting for the cleaning crew to finish in the room.

The kid was young, couldn't have been more than twenty-two or twenty-three years old. Nick found himself wondering what had happened to bring the kid to the hospital when he noticed the lack of a bump under the covers where his left leg should have been.

His heart took a nosedive. Oh, man. The kid had lost his leg.

Nick swallowed his pity and nodded at the boy. "I'm Dr Tremayne. How are you?"

"Fine." The kid's monotone voice and the way he stared at the ceiling over his head convinced Nick he was anything but fine. Nick hesitated for a moment, torn by indecision, then continued on his way to the nurses' station.

"What's the name of the new patient?" he asked the first nurse he saw.

"Hmm. You must mean Billy Anderson." The nurse wearing a nametag with the name of Margaret gestured toward a stack of paperwork. "Here's all his information from the floor if you need to review his case."

"Thanks." Nick stared at the stack of papers with dread. Billy's diagnosis jumped out at him: left leg amputation as a result of a motorcycle crash. He clenched his jaw. Abby was wrong, working rehab wasn't his kind of expertise at all. The last thing he wanted to do was to talk to this kid, this Billy Anderson, who had every right to be angry at the world.

He knew just how the kid felt.

Nick glanced over his shoulder in time to see a nurse's aide push Billy's cart into his room. The kid continued to stare at the ceiling, acting as if he couldn't care less which room they stuck him in. The expression of tense hopelessness struck a resonant chord.

Grabbing the sheaf of papers, he nodded at the nurse. "I'll be in the dictation room if you need me." Nick made his way to the privacy of the back dictation area then settled in to review Billy's past medical history and current level of care.

Fifteen minutes later, he shoved the information aside and scrubbed his hands over his face. Billy's story was similar in many ways to his own. A freak of fate and, wham, the kid finds himself in the hospital minus one leg.

With an effort, he forced himself to stand. If Roland hadn't completed the admission assessment on Billy, he'd need to call him on the discrepancy and complete it himself. No matter how difficult it would be.

"Which nurse is taking care of the new patient, Billy Anderson?" he asked Betty, seated behind the computer.

"Margaret is his nurse, she's in the room with him now," Betty replied.

"Has anyone done his admission assessment?"

Betty's eyes widened. "I thought Dr Roland did it earlier?"

Now it was his turn to be surprised. "Roland was here?"

She nodded. "Yes, but he didn't stay long. Just mentioned something about going up to complete the admission assessment on the new transfer, then he left. Billy Anderson is the only new patient we're scheduled to receive today."

A cowardly relief swept through him. At least he wouldn't have to face that poor kid. "Thanks for letting me know." He hadn't seen the information from Roland in the chart, but maybe it hadn't been transcribed yet. He paused, then asked, "Did Roland seem all right?"

"He was the same as usual, rude and short-tempered." She shrugged and turned her attention to the ringing phone.

There was no way he could ask if she'd specifically smelled alcohol on Roland's breath—those sorts of questions would only result in the spreading of nasty rumors. As much as he didn't care for Roland, especially after the scene he'd witnessed with Abby, encouraging speculation wouldn't be fair. Nick turned and left the unit.

Roland probably didn't have a drinking problem at all. He'd made the decision to stay in Milwaukee for nothing. In fact, Roland had everything under control on the unit this morning.

Outside, the hot summer sun beat down on his head. Last night he'd promised to call Abby, but now he hesitated. As much as he wanted to be with her, he knew the temptation was dangerous. One kiss goodnight and he'd almost dragged her back to his motel room for far more.

He didn't blame her brother the cop for being concerned. Abby was young, innocent and had her whole life ahead of her. She wanted to travel, to experience life at its fullest, and she deserved to do exactly that. His hand tightened on his cane. What could he offer her?

Especially now, when he had a very different mindset. He needed a place to settle down. A place to start over.

A place to find himself.

"Nick?" Abby's voice called to him and for a moment he wondered if he was dreaming. "I've been looking for you all morning."

Dressed in a pair of tiny denim shorts and a blue crop top, she looked adorable, both cute and sexy. He felt the tightness in his chest ease. Simply gazing at her made him feel young. Healthy. Ready to take on the world.

For a moment, Billy's stark image invaded his mind. He shoved it away.

"I went to do some therapy, then checked things out on the unit." He grinned when she approached. "You'll be glad to know Roland was in earlier this morning, actually making rounds."

"No." Her blue eyes widened. "I don't believe it."

"It's true." He held up a hand. "Scout's honor."

"You were a Scout?" Skepticism filled her tone. "Somehow I have trouble picturing you wearing the little blue uniform."

He laughed. "All right, you win. I was never a Scout. But I wasn't lying about Roland. Betty saw him making rounds."

"I'm glad. So are you finished for the day? Because if so, let's go."

"Where?"

"To German Fest, silly." Abby raked a critical gaze over his casual pants and collared shirt. "I'll wait while you change."

He had no idea what German Fest was, but the image

of beer-guzzling men shouting "Gemutliechkeit" came to mind. Not usually his thing but so what? Spending time with Abby was worth any price. The logical side of his head told him to decline her offer, to stay far away from her until it was time to book himself another flight back to Virginia.

Instead, he heard himself answer, "Sure. I'll be right back."

Abby sneaked several glances at Nick as they walked through the lakefront festival grounds. She'd borrowed Alec's car. It didn't come close to payback for his rude behavior but it was a start, and the ride downtown had been quiet. She'd gotten the distinct impression Nick wouldn't have called if she hadn't looked for him.

Uncertainty gnawed at her. Was she pushing? Maybe. Although maybe Nick just needed a few hours of fun. She was more than happy to oblige.

"What are they eating?" Nick asked when he saw several men walking by with huge bratwursts slathered with sauerkraut.

"Usinger's famous sausage." Her mouth watered at the pungent scent. "I'm hungry. Come on, you can't knock German sausage until you try some."

Nick paid for two sausages, then continued to stare at his meal with a doubtful expression. She grinned and took a big bite of her own bratwurst. "Mmm. I haven't had one of these in ages."

"I've never had one." Bravely, he took a bite and his skeptical expression cleared. "Hey, this is good."

"Told you." She walked toward the one of the stages

where dancers were assembled. The bright blue and green costumes flared when one of the girls twirled experimentally. "Isn't this great?"

"I've never seen anything like it," Nick allowed. She noticed he'd finished his entire bratwurst and still looked with interest at other people's food. "Do you have festivals like this all summer?"

"Yep. Festa Italiana, Irish Fest, Polish Fest, Mexican Festia." She ticked them off her fingers. "You name it, we have it."

They wandered around the fairgrounds, listening to a variety of folk music and trying different types of German food.

"I wouldn't mind trying a mug of the dark German beer," Nick admitted, after finishing off some schnitzel and licking his fingers in appreciation.

"Go ahead. I'm driving, remember?"

As dusk fell, they made their way closer to the lakefront. Nick had finished his beer and appeared to be feeling very mellow.

"We need to find a good spot." Abby scanned the grassy area intently. Several yards away, she noticed a perfect area partially hidden by an outcropping of rocks.

"For?" Nick raised a brow.

"To see the fireworks." She tugged on his arm. "This way, where there are fewer people."

"You're going to be cold in that outfit," he warned, as she led the way on a zig-zagging path through other onlookers.

"Phooey. Once we've claimed our squatters' rights, I'll go back to Alec's car and get a blanket." She sent a sly grin at him over her shoulder. "Do you think I'm a rookie?"

"Guess not."

Once she'd gotten Nick settled in the spot where she wanted to sit, she fetched him another of his dark German beers, then headed back to Alec's car. She decided against grabbing a sweatshirt but picked up Alec's oversized blanket then rooted through the glovebox. She walked back to Nick, only to discover he had a good beer buzz going.

"Hey." She frowned when he flashed her a goofy grin. "I bet you shouldn't be drinking with the medication you're on."

"Nah, I didn't take any pain meds today." He waved off her concern. Once she'd spread out the blanket, he stretched out and patted the ground beside him. "Come and sit here by me."

Having her way with Nick while he was under the influence wasn't part of her plan, but seeing him so relaxed and playful made it difficult to stay mad. She sat on the ground beside him and curled her arms around her knees for warmth as she gazed out at the lake. "It's so peaceful here."

"Beautiful." Nick propped himself on his good elbow and nuzzled her neck. "I'm the luckiest guy here."

She had to laugh at the slight slur in his words. "You're one of the tipsiest guys here."

Just then she heard a poofing sound and the first firecracker shot into the sky. Abby held her breath while the purple and green mushroom exploded in the sky with a bang.

"Wow." Nick was impressed enough to lift his head from her neck.

There was another muffled sound as a firecracker was lit. A showering of bright red and white sparkles bloomed in the sky. One by one, the fireworks went off as Abby and Nick huddled in the warmth of the blanket and watched.

The grand finale was breathtaking, dozens of fireworks exploding at once in a dazzling array of color. When the last of the booming echoes died down, the audience whistled and applauded the show.

Abby didn't make any attempt to move, though, she was far too comfortable stretched out beneath the blanket with the rocks sheltering their backs, tucked in the curve of Nick's arm.

"How long can we stay here?" Nick's deep voice rumbled in her ear. She tuned out the chatter of the people clearing the lakefront site.

"As long as we want, I guess." She tipped her head and pressed a soft kiss to his neck. He smelled wonderful, a perfect blend of spicy aftershave, beer and his own unique scent. The other men in her life paled in comparison to Nick. Even Shane.

Especially Shane. Looking back now, she realized her feelings toward him had been more friendship than anything else.

"Abby," he warned, when she tugged the neck of his T-shirt aside and boldly trailed kisses down toward his collar-bone. "We need to go."

Gradually, festival patrons left the grassy embankment, leaving them alone. Even better, they were far away from her family. Selfishly, she wanted to hang onto this moment and cherish it for ever.

"Not yet." The night air coming off Lake Michigan was cool, the rhythmic slurping of waves over the shore gave her a sense of peace. An assurance that being here with Nick was right.

For a moment she buried her face in the crook of his neck, inhaling deeply. His hands came up, lightly stroking her back, sliding up along the curve of her shoulder, then down over her hip. Over and over again until his hand lingered, his fingers tracing the edge of her cut-off shorts in a tentative motion, then caressing the bare skin of her thighs.

Her breathing quickened and her muscles tensed. Oh, yes. She wanted this. And more.

Lifting her head, she kissed his neck, then explored every inch she could reach, his face, his shoulder, trying to tell him without words what she wanted.

He must have finally gotten the message because all too soon he captured her mouth in a deep, probing kiss.

She opened to him, welcoming him in. With an abrupt movement he turned her so she was half-pinned beneath him. She reveled in the hardness of his body pressing against her. They could have the only two people left on the planet earth for all she cared. The outcropping of rocks added a sense of isolation from the world.

Abby gasped when Nick slid his hand along the skin of her belly, then further still until his fingers were splayed beneath her thin top.

She longed to get rid of the barrier of clothing. Her top had a built-in bra and she ached for him to touch her. As if he sensed her every whim, he withdrew his hand and slowly slid the straps of her tank down, baring her breasts.

"So beautiful." He spoke in a reverent tone. "You're killing me, Abby."

Not half as much as he was killing her. No one had ever made her feel like this. Sexy. Special. Desired. Loved.

"Please?" She arched her back, pulling him closer. He lowered his head and dragged his tongue in a light caress across one distended nipple.

Sensation spiraled through her, time hung suspended as if there was only this moment and nothing else. With impatient hands she stripped his shirt from his back and swept her hands over his back, feeling the taut muscles then delving lower in the small indentation beyond the waistband of his jeans. She didn't notice when the breeze picked up. Beneath the blanket they generated more than enough heat to stay warm.

Hampered by the blanket, Nick awkwardly peeled off the rest of her clothes, then pulled off his jeans. She giggled as they bumped elbows and knees, but when they were both finally naked, the feel of his hard body pressed against hers stole her breath. He stared down at her, although she couldn't see much of his expression in the darkness of the night.

"Abby, I didn't bring protection."

"I did." She held up a condom and pressed it into his hand. At least there was one perk from having four older brothers. True to form, Alec had a secret stash in his car.

"Are you sure about this?" Every muscle in his body was tense as he held himself in check. She liked it better when he was holding her, touching her, kissing her.

Was he looking for a way out?

She wished she could see him more clearly. But indecisive she wasn't. Sliding her hands up his shoulders, she nodded. "Yes. I'm sure."

He took a moment to protect her, then began all over again, kissing every inch of her body like she'd explored his. Until she couldn't take another moment of the sweet torture. She pulled him down, wrapping her legs around his waist. With a low groan, he slid deep.

Pleasure spiked and she thought it was a miracle they didn't self-combust right then. He moved slowly, deliberately and with a small cry she raised her hips to meet each thrust.

"Abby. Dear, sweet Abby." He murmured words of love, of caring as he quickened his pace, taking her higher, to places she'd never seen, never known.

"Nick!" She cried his name as her body exploded into a quivering mass of sensation. He surged against her and she held him close, nearly dying with pleasure.

For long moments Nick's ragged breathing filled her ears. When he began to pull away, she made a desperate grab for him.

"Don't go," she murmured.

He pressed a kiss on her forehead. Her cheek. Her mouth. "Sweetheart, my arm won't hold my weight much longer."

Good heavens, she'd almost forgotten his injuries. She struggled upright, pushing at him until he rolled onto his back.

"Don't even ask," he warned, as if sensing her concerned expression. "I'm great. Wonderful. Ecstatic."

She had to laugh. "OK, I won't." Although she couldn't help but worry. Smoothing a hand down his body, she felt the ridges of his scars along his hip, but thankfully no muscle spasms.

"I'm so happy." She pressed a kiss over the area above his heart, grinning at him like a fool in the dark. "Do you think anyone would notice if we stayed here all night?"

"Oh, yeah, I'm sure Alec would find us." Nick's tone was dry. "Let's not chance fate, all right?"

"I have to admit, I'm pretty amazed no one has called." Under the protection of the blanket, Abby reached for her purse to check her phone. "Oops. Guess I left my cell phone off."

"Didn't you do that last night, too?" Nick's voice was lazy. "I think they're on to your tricks."

She turned her phone on, not surprised to see there were at least four messages. She sighed. Why wouldn't her family just leave her alone?

She was tempted to toss it aside, not willing to give up this time alone with Nick. But she realized most of the messages were from her sister, Alaina.

Not her brothers. Or her parents. But Alaina.

Strange.

"Hey." Nick struggled upright, clutching the blanket tighter around them as one end started to slip from her shoulders. "We'd better get dressed before someone sees us."

She set her phone aside long enough to pull on her clothes, then picked it up again to listen to the first message.

"Abby, Bethany was hit by a car. They took her to Children's." Her sister's sobbing voice filled her ears. "Where are you? Please, call me. I need you."

"No! Oh, God." Horrified, she threw the blanket aside and surged to her feet. "Hurry. Beth is hurt!"

CHAPTER TWELVE

NICK knew Abby had been upset after finding out Mr Goetz had died, but this situation hit far closer to home. He insisted on driving Abby to the hospital and it was a testimony as to how distraught she was that she didn't argue. Frantic, she listened to her phone messages while he negotiated traffic.

"Any more information?" he asked when she snapped her phone shut.

"No." She clamped her lower lip between her teeth. "I can't believe I left my phone off. My sister sounded awful. Poor Beth. Oh, Nick, what if she's really hurt? I can't stand it. Please, hurry."

"Don't think the worst." Nick pushed the speed limit as much as he dared. "I'm sure she's going to be fine."

"You don't know that." Abby stared out the window, her jaw tight. "She's only six years old. Good grief, she's only a baby." Her voice broke.

Nick captured her hand in his, holding tight. He didn't know what to say, so he fell silent. For all Abby's tough talk about moving away, she was still very close to her family. How would she cope if this had happened while she'd been in Florida? He couldn't imagine.

For any child hit by a car, the odds weren't good. Still, there were many factors to be considered. Had the child been hit as a pedestrian? Or while riding a bike? Had she been wearing a helmet? Had the car only clipped her or hit directly head on?

As part of his trauma training, he'd done a stint at Children's Memorial. The number of kids hit by cars while riding their bikes was phenomenal. The ones injured worst hadn't been wearing their helmets. If Beth had been on a bike, he prayed she'd been wearing some type of headgear.

He pulled into the parking lot at Children's Memorial and circled around to the emergency entrance. The car wasn't even at a complete stop when Abby leapt out and flew inside.

Nick followed at his slower pace, feeling guilty for the role he'd played in keeping her out of contact with her family. Those stolen moments they'd shared beneath the blanket at the lakefront had been the most wonderful of his life. Totally mind-boggling.

But there wasn't time to dwell on the pleasure. Only the aftermath of pain.

The Monroe family took up at least half of the waiting room. As Nick approached, he noticed Abby's brother, Adam, the pediatric doctor wasn't there. There was one other brother—Aaron, he thought—who also wasn't around. Alaina was in the middle of the group, holding on to her toddler son and rocking back and forth, looking as if she was in shock.

No surprise there.

Abby knelt beside her sister and engulfed her in a hug. Nick stopped just outside the family circle, straining to overhear.

"What happened? How is she? What are they doing for her?" Abby fired questions faster than a Marine drill sergeant.

"She has a compound fracture in her right leg, they're talking about taking her to surgery." Alaina sniffled and swiped at her eyes. "She was riding her bike in the driveway, I always tell her not to go into the road, but she went out in the road to make a wide turn and Mr Green, the neighbor across the street, was backing out of his driveway and didn't see her. Luckily, he wasn't going very fast."

"And she was wearing her helmet, right?" Abby brushed a kiss across Ben's forehead.

"Yes." Alaina's voice was faint, rough along the edges from bouts of crying. "We've been here in the ED for hours, they're short on beds apparently. Adam's in there with her now while they prepare her for surgery. Ben was crying, so Dad came in to get me."

"I'll sit here with Ben, you go back in with Beth." Abby's tone was firm and she took the child from her sister's lap and hugged him close. Nick expected the kid to protest but he didn't seem to mind.

Alaina left to return to her daughter. Nick debated whether or not he should just leave now that Abby was ensconced with her family, but just then Alec sidled up beside him. "Thanks for bringing Abby. We were worried when she didn't answer her phone."

Nick stifled a surge of impatience. He wasn't the

phone police, but he could understand their concern. "We went to German Fest. Watched the fireworks."

Alec didn't so much as smile. "Guess she couldn't hear her phone over the noise, huh?"

"She had her phone off." Nick didn't see the need to lie. "Maybe because you guys are just a little over-protective." He shrugged. "But, hey, I don't mind. I told Abby I thought it was nice, the way you guys looked after her."

With a scowl Alec turned and glanced at his sister. "I'm not trying to be nice."

"Yeah, that's what she said, too." Nick followed Alec's gaze, then sucked in a quick breath. Cuddling Ben, Abby wore a nurturing expression that he could easily envision her bestowing on her own child. His child. Their child.

Wait a minute, where did that thought come from?

He wasn't ready to have kids, not by a long shot. At the moment he couldn't even support himself. Nick swallowed hard and glanced away. He wasn't ready for children, but if he did decide to have them, he couldn't imagine a better mother than Abby.

"I have to go." He dug Abby's keys out of his pocket and handed them to Alec. "Give these to Abby, would you?"

Alec seemed to sense his unease and a small smile tugged at the corner of his mouth. "How are you going to get back?"

Nick shrugged. "I'll call a cab."

"I'll drive you. I have a police cruiser parked outside." Alec leaned over to his brother Austin, who was sitting beside Abby, and said something in a low tone, before gesturing to the door. "Let's go."

Hesitant, Nick glanced at Abby, but she was preoccupied between the child in her arms, her other brothers and her parents hovering around her. They were deep in conversation and he didn't think it was prudent to interrupt. This was family. He had no business being here. Swallowing his desire to kiss her senseless, he turned and followed Alec outside.

"So, tell me more about this guy Roland." Alec turned down the volume of his police radio as he pulled out into the traffic. "Where can I find him?"

"At the hospital." Nick raised a brow. "You can't do anything about him if Abby won't press charges."

"Actually, that depends on what he did to her." Alec sent Nick an enigmatic sidelong glance. "What happened?"

Nick explained the brief altercation. When he finished, Alec was scowling.

"I can't believe it!" Alec thumped a hand on the steering-wheel. "Why in the blazes wouldn't she press charges? The guy's a menace."

Considering how much he'd wanted to press charges himself, he knew how her brother felt. Still, now he wasn't so sure. Hadn't Roland come in that morning to make rounds? Maybe the guy was just going through a bad time. "He'll likely leave her alone now." Nick grinned. "You'll be glad to know I did mention Abby's brother was a cop."

"Good." Alec didn't so much as crack a smile. "What's his first name? I'll run him through the system, see what pops out."

"Douglas."

Alec nodded and pulled into the parking lot of the motel. "Thanks."

"You're welcome." Nick was surprised Abby's brother hadn't continued to grill him over what he and Abby had been doing. He tried to climb out of the car, but the ache in his leg intensified to the point he couldn't bear much weight. This was the price he'd paid by not taking any pain meds. It galled him to show his weakness before Abby's brother, but it would have been far worse if Alec had offered to get out and help him. Gripping the door with one hand and the frame overhead with the other, Nick swallowed a groan and pulled himself upright.

Darkness blurred his vision and for a moment he slumped against the door. When he heard Alec's car door open, he gathered himself together with an effort.

"Need a hand?" Alec offered, his previous hostility gone.

Shame crawled up the back of Nick's neck, settling on his shoulders like a living, breathing beast. "No."

Although it cost him, Nick forced himself to lean heavily on his cane, then against the wall of the building as he made his way to his room. Alec walked behind him, as if waiting for him to fall. Not until Nick was all the way inside the door did Alec climb back into his cruiser and drive away.

Alec's protective attitude scraped on Nick's ego like nails over an open wound. He didn't need a damn babysitter making sure he got home all right. For a moment he shared a spurt of sympathy for Abby. No wonder her family drove her nuts.

Inside his motel room, he collapsed onto the bed. The fiery pain in his leg throbbed, and he took several deep breaths in a vain attempt to control the sharp edges curling around his mind.

Only once the pain receded did he allow himself to drift back to those moments he'd held Abby in his arms. To relive the sensation when their bodies had become one.

His chest tightened and his eyes flew open in alarm as the realization hit.

He loved her.

He wasn't sure how it had happened, or why. But he'd fallen in love with Abby Monroe.

For an instant he thought of Shane. Had Shane loved Abby? He thought back over her letters. No, from what he remembered, theirs had been just the early stages of a relationship.

Shane hadn't loved Abby. At least, not with the same depth he did. He loved her with his whole heart and soul.

But that didn't mean she felt the same way about him.

Clamping his eyes shut, he forced himself to shove the dazzling feelings aside. No matter how much it hurt inside, she was in a different place in her life.

He wouldn't only think about himself, not any more.

He had to love her enough to let her go.

Abby knew guilt was making her a little irrational, but she refused to leave the hospital until Beth was safe at home. Although she was more than a little perturbed at how Nick had left without saying goodbye. She wanted to call him, but she wanted to stay with her family more.

So she waited. Until the orthopedic surgeon had repaired Beth's open tibia fracture. Until a couple of hours later, when a drowsy Beth had returned to her room, her left leg in a cast.

Although Alaina tried several times to get her to leave, she just couldn't do it. Every time she considered going home, she would remember exactly what she and Nick had been doing while Alaina had left frantic messages on her cell phone. In truth, Alaina had called far earlier in the evening. Beth had been hit at seven-thirty p.m. But still, she couldn't seem to separate the fact that she hadn't been there for Beth when she'd been hurt because she'd been too busy making love with Nick.

She slept on a cot in Beth's room. The doctor released Beth the next afternoon, Sunday. Abby went over to Alaina's house to make sure Beth was settled in and comfortable then she helped entertain Ben so Alaina could prepare something for dinner.

Using his red and blue building blocks, she made a tower, smiling ruefully when Ben swatted it down. As she played with Ben, she wondered what Nick was doing. Had he packed up his duffel bag and checked out? Hopped a plane back to Virginia? Did he miss her? Did he regret making love under a blanket of stars?

She didn't know what was going through his mind. All she knew was that he hadn't called. What if he really had left town?

The thought of not seeing him ever again made her stomach twist and turn like a pretzel.

By Monday, Abby was torn as to whether or not she

LAURA IDING

should still plan on giving her notice. Not because she'd changed her mind about leaving, but because of what had transpired with Nick. He'd seemed concerned about Beth, but then had left Abby at the hospital without bothering to stop by the next day to see how Beth was doing.

Granted, he was still torn up inside about the loss of his career, and she understood how difficult it must be. Even if he had left town, wouldn't he at least have tried to call?

Pushing irritating thoughts of Nick from her mind, Abby went to work first thing Monday morning. She discovered they had a new patient, a young man by the name of Billy Anderson, who had suffered a traumatic leg amputation from a motorcycle crash.

"Good morning, Billy. My name is Abby, I'll be your nurse today."

Silence. Billy lay flat on his back, staring blankly at the ceiling over his head. He acted as if he hadn't heard her.

"Billy, you're scheduled to go downstairs for physical therapy at nine. Do you want to shower before or after therapy?"

More silence. The flat expression in his eyes sent alarm bells ringing through her head.

Billy was depressed. Seriously depressed. Worse than the patient who'd killed himself after being discharged.

Abby squared her jaw. Nothing like that was going to happen to Billy. Not if she had anything to do about it.

She told Billy she'd be back later. After leaving his room, she reviewed his chart. She was glad to see the trauma team had placed him on antidepressants and, miracle of all miracles, Roland had even reordered the medication here on rehab. She counted back the days since they'd been started, back on the acute care unit. Two weeks.

She frowned. The medication either wasn't working or hadn't kicked in yet.

Or Billy was faking swallowing them.

Abby gnawed her lip. She wished Nick were still in town. Billy needed someone to talk to, someone like Nick who knew what it was like to suffer a traumatic event. They had plenty of psychologists on staff, but most of them were older. She sensed Billy would respond better to someone younger.

If anyone could get through his stubborn silence, Nick could.

She hoped.

When she returned to the nurses' station, Abby was surprised to see Dr Roland seated at a computer, reading a chart.

"Good morning, Dr Roland." She strove to be polite, although the dark bruises still hadn't faded from her wrist and knee.

"Hrmph." He didn't tear his gaze from the screen.

She edged closer, trying to ascertain if there was any smell of alcohol. She couldn't smell anything until she was standing right over his shoulder. And even then the odor was faint.

"I need to ask you about Billy Anderson." Her excuse

for coming so close. Anxiously, Abby glanced around. She didn't want to be the only person who smelled alcohol on the guy. Where was everyone? She couldn't trust her nose to be impartial.

"What about him?" When he turned toward her, the scent of alcohol was stronger. Roland's brusque attitude didn't soften, as if she was the one who'd wronged him. What a laugh.

"He's very depressed. I think he needs to have the rehab psychiatrist talk to him."

"Fine. I'll order a consult." With that, Roland stood and moved to walk around her.

Wait! she wanted to cry out, to stop him from leaving. Then she saw Irene walking down the hallway and hurried over.

"Irene, I need you to go over by Roland, tell me if you smell anything funny."

The nurse wrinkled her brow. "What do you mean? Why would he smell funny?"

She didn't want to give away her suspicions. "Please? Just go over and ask him a question."

"All right." Irene turned and headed down the hall. "Dr Roland? I have a quick question."

Abby watched as the two of them spoke for a moment before Roland broke away to go into one of the patient's rooms. Irene came back toward her.

"Well?" Abby grabbed her arm. "What do you think?"

"I don't think anything." Irene shrugged off her hand. "Maybe he had a little too much to drink last night, that doesn't mean he's impaired."

"So you did smell the alcohol." Abby slumped with

relief. "It's not my imagination, then." Then she pro-
cessed what Irene had said. "Wait a minute. Of course
he might be impaired. We have to call Leanne."

"Oh, no, don't drag me into this." Irene lifted her
hands and backed off. "I didn't smell anything."

Abby's jaw dropped. What? She had to be kidding.
"Irene, this is serious. What if he makes a mistake?
Hurts someone? We can't ignore this."

"You may be leaving here soon, Abby, but I need this
job." Irene's worried gaze tore at her. "I just found out
I'm pregnant. I can't afford to get fired. I think he's fine.
There's nothing wrong with his medical decisions."
With one last glance over her shoulder, Irene hurried off.

Abby stared at her retreating figure with a sense of
doom. Roland was dangerous, she knew only too well
what happened when he had too much to drink. But if
she couldn't find someone to corroborate her story,
she'd be seen as a troublemaker. Leanne had already put
a counseling report in her file for being rude. Pursuing
this further could cost her her job. Although, as Irene
had pointed out, it didn't matter as she already had
another job lined up in Florida.

While she stood, torn by indecision, Roland came
out of the patient's room and headed toward her. Their
gazes locked and in that instant his tiny, smug smile sent
a shaft of fury sizzling through her nerves. He acted as
if he knew her days here were numbered and once she
was gone, he'd go right back to doing whatever he
wanted.

"Excuse me, Dr Roland. I need to have a word
with you." Abby heard the words come out of her

mouth and desperately wanted to call them back. What was she doing?

"Now what?" His smug smile vanished, replaced by intense irritation.

"I need you to talk to Leanne." She was winging it, she didn't know what else to do. "There seems to be an issue we need to resolve."

"I'm busy. Tell your boss I'll talk to her later." Roland brushed past her and in a few moments she knew her chance would be lost. Once he left the unit it would be too late.

"No, wait." Abby raised her voice when he continued to walk. "Dr Roland! Have you been drinking?" she blurted.

Someone on the other side of the nurses' station gasped. But she'd managed to get his attention. He spun around and marched back toward her.

"What did you say?" His voice was deceptively quiet, but the expression in his eyes shot fiery daggers, as if he wished nothing more than to see her burn in hell.

She didn't know what to do. For a long moment no one came to stand beside her. The two of them faced each other as if in a duel. Then, over Roland's shoulder, she saw Nick walking down the hall, leaning heavily on his cane.

Nick wouldn't let this go. She wasn't totally alone here after all. Thrusting her chin toward Roland in defiance, she tossed her head. "You heard me. I asked you a question. Have you been drinking? Because I smell alcohol on your breath."

When Roland stepped closer, she wanted very badly
to turn and run. But she wasn't expecting his hand to
swing toward her face until it cracked across her cheek.

CHAPTER THIRTEEN

UTTERLY demoralized, Abby stared at him as stinging pain blazed across her cheek. Before she could think of something to say, Nick rushed over.

"That's it, Roland. You've crossed the line this time." Nick's eyes widened as he drew close enough to smell him. "I don't believe it. You have been drinking!"

"I'm filing a formal complaint with Hospital Administration and the American Medical Association." Abby found her voice. She was glad Nick was there to smell the alcohol on Roland, but she also wasn't letting Roland off the hook so easily. Not this time. "For assault and for working under the influence."

"I'll be your witness, Abby." Irene came out from behind the nurses' station to stand beside her. A little late, but Abby understood Irene's position. Her unborn baby had to come first.

"Good. That makes three of us. I'll be a witness, too." Nick aligned himself with Abby, placing his body solidly in front of hers as protection. "Get out of here,

Roland. Now. You have no business taking care of patients in your condition."

Roland hesitated, then swung away and walked out of the unit. Abby brought a hand up to cover her flaming cheek. "Good riddance," she muttered.

"Here, let's get some ice for you." Nick's eyes were full of concern as he gently pulled her hand from her face.

"No, I'm fine." Abby shrugged off his grasp. "Thanks for coming over, Irene."

"I should have come sooner." The woman worried her lower lip between her teeth. "You were right, Abby. I'm sorry."

"Hey, don't worry. I understand." Abby wished she could turn back the clock and forget the whole ugly scene, but she was satisfied Roland was no longer a threat to his patients. With an effort she thought about what needed to be done.

"Are you sure you're all right?" Nick's eyes reflected doubt.

"I'm sure." An idea struck. "Would you do me a favor, though? Would you go and talk to one of my patients?"

"Sure. Who?"

"Billy Anderson."

"I'm not sure my talking to Billy will do any good." Nick's expression was grave. "He needs professional help."

"Maybe." She couldn't argue that one. "But I'm betting he's had professional help before on the floor. Maybe what he needs is unprofessional help from someone who's been there."

Resigned, Nick nodded. "I can try. What's going on? Did he refuse therapy?"

"He isn't co-operating with therapy, but that's only part of the problem. The real issue is he's depressed." Abby lowered her tone. "Just try to talk to him. Make him see he's not alone in this."

"All right." Nick blew out a breath. "Has Psych come to see him yet?"

"Not yet. Roland was just going to order the consult." Abby turned back toward the nurses' station. When she approached, Betty avoided her gaze.

She told herself she didn't care. Even though Roland was in the wrong, she was still *persona non grata* around here. She pulled up Billy's chart on the computer and was surprised to see Roland had, in fact, ordered the psych consult for Billy. Praying that somehow Nick would get through to the kid, she picked up the ringing phone since no one else was around.

"Rehab. This is Abby."

"Abby, I understand you're causing a little excitement in the unit." Leanne must have found out about Roland. Boy, bad news traveled fast.

"Yes, but Dr Tremayne and I both smelled the alcohol on his breath," Abby pointed out in her defense.

"I heard." Leanne's tone was dry. "Actually, Dr Johnson is already aware of the situation. Roland has been put on medical leave until further notice."

"Good." Abby sucked in a breath then made a quick decision. "Leanne, as long as you're on the phone, I'd like to move up my resignation date. My last day will be two weeks from today."

There was a long pause on the other end of the line. "I see. All right, I'll change your last day of employment with us for two weeks from today. I'm sorry to see you go, Abby."

"I'll miss you, too, Leanne. But thanks." As she hung up the phone, Abby felt overwhelming relief. At least now she could leave knowing Roland was no longer a threat.

She signed off Billy's chart and went to find Nick. She heard his deep voice coming from Billy's room. Pausing outside the door, she listened, not wanting to interrupt.

"I've been in your shoes—do you want me to prove it?" The rustle of clothing made her eyes widen. Was Nick really showing Billy his scars?

"So? A few measly scars isn't anything like losing a leg." Billy didn't sound impressed. "It's gone for ever."

"Yeah, but is a leg that doesn't work any better?" Nick argued in a calm, logical tone. "Would you be happier sitting in that chair with two paralyzed legs? Or even one paralyzed leg?"

There was a long moment of silence.

"Yeah, I didn't think so. Look around you, Billy. You'll always find people who are better off and worse off than you are. At this point all you can do is take the hand you were dealt and figure out what to do next. Are you going to fold? Or play the game? Are you willing to take another card? Rehab is another card, Billy. It's a chance to get back on your feet, even if one of them is a prosthesis."

Billy remained silent for so long Abby edged closer, ready to intervene if necessary.

"You really think there's a woman out there who will fall for a guy without a leg?" Billy asked in a low tone.

Oh, heavens. Abby's heart squeezed in her chest.

"I've found since my accident that women are better at overlooking our physical limitations than men are." Nick didn't brush off his concern or give him a line. "Will some women be turned off by it? Maybe. I won't lie to you. But I think women need emotional strength from a guy more than anything else. The toughest part is overcoming our own insecurities in order to provide it."

Another silence. "All right. I'll go to therapy."

Blinking away a stray tear, Abby swallowed hard. Billy would be all right. She was convinced he'd make it home.

"Good." More rustling as Nick pulled his shirt back on. "And, Billy? I'm here if you need to talk."

Abby wanted to linger and wait for Nick to thank him, but she needed to see to her other patients. Knowing she'd find him later, she hurried down the hall.

His words, though, echoed in her mind. *Women need emotional strength from a guy more than anything else. The toughest part is overcoming our insecurities in order to provide it.* Had Nick been referring to the two of them? Hope sprouted like new, green shoots from the depths of her heart. Was their relationship more important to him than she'd realized?

Nick left Billy's room to respond to a page from Rick Johnson. He glanced around for Abby, then heard her voice in another patient's room. He wanted to let her know about Billy, but first he'd better go and see Johnson.

He strode down to the administrative offices.

"Rick." Nick nodded at the chief of staff on entering his office. They shook hands. "What can I do for you?"

"Thought you should know, Roland refused to seek treatment for his alcohol problem." Rick sat back in his chair and tapped his fingertips together. "Which left me no choice but to fire him."

Nick couldn't summon any sympathy for Roland. Not after the way he'd slapped Abby. "Too bad."

"Yes, actually, it is." Rick frowned. "His wife died of cancer two years ago and he hasn't been the same since. I had hoped he'd come round after I gave him the responsibility of being the medical director. Despite everything these past few months, he was once a very good doctor."

Ah, damn. Nick rubbed his temple. He hadn't known anything about Roland's wife dying of cancer. Now he did feel sorry for the guy. A little, anyway. "There's still time for him to get help. I can try to talk to him."

Rick waved him off. "No, I'll talk to him. He's only going to see you as part of the problem. Besides, that's not why I asked you here."

Nick waited with patient curiosity. He couldn't imagine there was anything else to discuss.

"I spoke with your boss in Fairfax, Virginia," Rick surprised him by saying. "Stephen White is a big fan of yours. But he has some concerns about your ability to return to your previous position."

Opening and closing the fingers on his injured hand, Nick kept his expression impassive. "He has every reason to be concerned. I won't be able to perform surgery. Ever. Stephen is probably waiting for my resignation."

Rick nodded. "That's what I thought. Would you consider staying on here? I have an open Medical Director position to offer you."

Stunned, Nick stared at him. "I don't have the credentials to be the medical director of rehabilitation."

"Take the boards, you'll get them." Rick didn't seem too concerned. "With your trauma surgery background, it's not a stretch. These past few weeks have convinced me you're perfect for the job."

He didn't know what to do, or what to say. A part of him wanted to run, to get away from facing the truth. He'd always wanted to be a surgeon. Couldn't believe the career he'd loved had been snatched out of his reach.

Yet how much longer could he continue to fool himself into believing otherwise? The incident with the central line had convinced him his career was finished.

Despite himself, Johnson's offer created a flicker of interest. Maybe he didn't really know much about physical medicine but he did know what it was like to be a rehab patient. His little chat with Billy hadn't been as awful as he'd thought it would be. As the person in charge, there were things he could do around here to help.

He warmed to the idea. Why couldn't he take the boards? And staying on here would give him a place, a purpose. He'd lived while Shane had died, but his life was worth something.

What about Abby? She wanted to travel, to see the world, but her family was here. Maybe she would consider staying?

No, that wasn't fair. Abby had to make her own decisions, and so did he. This decision had to be about him. His life. His career.

"All right." A sense of rightness swept over him as he accepted the position. "I'll take your offer, Rick."

"Great." Johnson grinned. "I've asked Cathy, Roland's former assistant, to clean his personal stuff out of his office so you can move in." He picked up a key from his desk and tossed it at Nick. "She'll have the office ready for you within the hour."

Nick closed his hand around the key and stood. There was still time to back out, to change his mind, but he knew he wouldn't. "I'll find out when I can take the boards."

"I know you will." Johnson didn't look worried. "I'm glad you're staying, Nick. You were a great consultant. I think you're going to be a better medical director."

With a nod, Nick left. In a daze, he returned to the rehab unit. When he saw Billy, seated in his wheelchair with his prosthetic leg on, wheeling himself down toward the elevators for his scheduled session in the physical therapy gym, he knew he'd made the right choice.

For him.

A few hours later he was seated in his new office, facing a mass of paperwork that needed to be taken care of. Roland hadn't done much of anything over the past few months.

One item in particular caught his eye, a request for a professional reference from Traveling Nurses, Inc. for Abigail Monroe.

Cathy poked her head in the door. "I've had several

messages from that traveling nurse company. Apparently they really need that reference."

He stared at the request in his hand. And if he didn't fill it out? Then what? He shook his head. Abby would still go. She'd find someone else to give her a professional reference. Besides, this needed to be her choice, not his.

"I'll get this completed a.s.a.p.," Nick promised. Shoving the rest of the pile aside, he booted up the computer and prepared a glowing reference for Abby.

He'd just finished printing the letter out when Cathy called from her desk in the outer office.

"Yeah?"

"There's a nurse here to see you, Abby Monroe."

His pulse quickened. "Send her in."

Abby stormed through the doorway. "I didn't believe it when Leanne told me."

He stood. "It's true."

"You took Roland's job!" she accused.

"Yeah."

"But I've already given my notice."

The letter burned in his hand. "I know."

"And that's all you can say to me? Don't you care?"

He cared, more than she'd ever know. He loved her. But he couldn't be the reason she stayed, she had to figure things out for herself. His hopes and dreams crumbled into tiny pieces.

"I care, Abby." He willed her to see the truth. "But working with Billy made me realize how right you were. This is my job now, assisting other rehab patients like myself. I can't be the world traveler you need."

"Don't ask me to stay here, because I can't." She

spun away from him, rubbing her hands over her bare arms. "I've never been outside Wisconsin. All my life I've dreamed of traveling—of seeing the world. I have to go somewhere. Anywhere." She whirled back to face him. "I'm happy you've decided to try rehab but you can practice anywhere. We can go to Virginia. Or somewhere else. I don't care. You pick the place and we'll go."

"I'm not leaving, Abby." Nick recoiled from the anguish he saw reflected in her eyes. For the first time he realized she really did care for him, for Nick Tremayne. With all his faults and scars. But he couldn't change himself just to make her happy. "I've made my decision to stay. But I think you should travel, if that's what you want. Just make sure you're not going for the wrong reasons."

"What wrong reasons? Because it's always been my dream?" Her tone held an unusual bitterness.

"No. Because you're using your desire to travel as an excuse to escape your family."

"That's not it at all." Abby threw her hands up. "Trust me, Nick, leaving my family is only an added benefit. The confetti sprinkles on top of my ice-cream cone of independence. Traveling is what I've always wanted to do."

The letters she'd written to Shane had stressed that very thing. And he knew she deserved to have this time to herself. To see the world. There was no use trying to talk her out of it, any more than he'd reconsider his position. They stood, with a wide chasm between them.

With a horrible sense of doom, he handed the letter to her. "The traveling nurse company called. They have a hold on your position because they needed one more professional reference. You'll be happy to know I completed it for you. Your job in Florida is safe."

She took the letter from his hand and frowned down at it for a long moment. "You wrote me a letter of recommendation?" Her voice was dull, flat. Too much like Billy's had been. "I thought you cared about me?"

"I do."

"Then how can you ask me to leave?"

"How can you ask me to do the same?"

A dull, heavy silence fell between them.

Nick couldn't stand it any more. He forced himself to sound enthused. "Hey, stop looking so glum. You just said how this is your dream. I understand." He remembered how excitement had hummed through his system when he'd been offered the chance to do his special training program in Beijing. He couldn't steal that thrill from her, now or ever.

Because he loved her too much.

He stood, helpless to do anything but convince her to go. "I'll be here when you come home for visits. But if you're asking my advice, I'd say you should go to Florida. I think it's important to follow your dream."

CHAPTER FOURTEEN

FLORIDA at the very end of July was suffocatingly hot. Humidity bloated the air and thick dark clouds loomed ominously low on the horizon. Swaying palm trees towered over the dull gray ribbon of highway. Abby peered through the window of the back seat of her taxi, anxious to wallow in the ambience of every sight and every sound.

She didn't want to admit her keen disappointment on discovering that, aside from the scrub brush, palm trees, lack of green grass, and if you didn't count the golf courses and stucco single-story houses, there wasn't much to distinguish Fort Meyers from Milwaukee.

With an irritated sigh, she shoved the thought aside. There were plenty of different experiences in Florida. Like the people, for one. Her cab driver was a perfect example, a huge guy with dreadlocks who loved to chat. The pawnshops on every corner, for another. She was certain that if she tried, she'd find all kinds of excitement here.

Like the impending storm. They had summer thunderstorms in Milwaukee, too, but not during the past sunny, drought-ridden month. Maybe storms were more impressive here, so close to the ocean. She leaned forward to get the cab driver's attention. "Does it rain here often?"

"Every day." Her eyes widened in horror. A white smile flashed in his dark face. "It's our rainy season. The day generally starts out fair and sunny, but every afternoon the stormclouds move in off the ocean and we get a nasty rainstorm. But the weather blows over in a few hours."

"How long is your rainy season?"

The cabbie shrugged then shouted, "Hey!" and leaned on his horn when someone started to move into his lane. Abby tugged on her seat belt to ensure it was securely fastened. Lightning rippled across the sky. Booming thunder followed several seconds later. "Depends, but the rain extends through September and October, the height of our hurricane season."

"Oh. Great." She sank into her seat with a weak smile. Hurricane season. Of course. Living through a hurricane would be exciting.

Maybe.

She closed her eyes and tried to summon her enthusiasm. At least she was here, in Fort Meyers, Florida, with her boxes of belongings scheduled to arrive in the next couple of days. She couldn't wait to unpack. Her first plane ride had been uneventful, but she'd gripped the seat arms tight as they'd taken off because her mind had conjured up images of Nick and Shane's plane crash.

Nick. Her chest tightened, stinging with shards of

regret. She hadn't seen him in over a week. The rumor going around the hospital had been that he'd left to take care of his own move from Virginia to Wisconsin.

She'd honestly thought he really cared for her. Maybe even had started to fall in love with her. The way she had fallen in love with him. Right before he'd written a glowing letter of recommendation on her behalf. Sure, he cared about her.

Not.

What a fool she'd been. How ridiculous to confuse love with lust. Just because they'd made love huddled in a blanket on the shores of Lake Michigan, it didn't mean anything.

Except that Nick had been horny and she'd been convenient.

The cabbie pulled into the driveway leading to her condo complex. Fat drops of rain began to splat on the windshield.

"Thanks so much." She paid her fare and jumped out, dragging the single carry-on suitcase behind her. One step later, the sky opened up in earnest and buckets of water dumped onto her head.

"Darn it!" Ducking her face to avoid the water, she ran up to the second-story condo doorway and crowded as close to the door as she could to stay out of the slanting rain. Not that it mattered much. Her clothes were already plastered to her skin.

Inside, the air smelled stale and musty. She opened the windows a few inches, then glanced around her new home.

A plethora of seashells decorated the walls and dotted the expanse of polyester bedspreads. The neutral earth tones and endless beach motif grated on her nerves. Maybe once she'd earned her first paycheck, she'd go shopping and pick out some things in bright, bold colors. And once her stuff arrived, and she'd put her pictures of her family around to feel more at home, she'd feel better.

Thinking about her family, she pulled out her cell phone and turned it on, expecting to see a slew of messages from her parents, her brothers and Alaina.

But there wasn't a single one.

Her shoulders slumped as she sank down on the edge of the bed. All right, she was off to a slow start and the rain pelting on her windows didn't help her dismal mood. But there was no reason to sit here and second-guess her decisions. Heck, she hadn't even given her new home a fair chance.

No way was she going to call her family. This was exactly what she'd wanted, to be left alone. To be independent.

To follow her dream of exploring the world, one state at a time.

Alone. The word had never sounded so pitiful.

Nick watched Billy work in the physical therapy gym with a sense of satisfaction. The kid was really coming along. He worked with the equipment as if he were on a mission to get out of here.

He didn't blame the kid. He knew exactly how Billy felt. Those months he'd spent in rehab had been the longest of his life.

Nick returned to his office and the stack of paperwork

awaiting his attention. One thing he'd learned, a medical director position involved far more paperwork than he'd ever dreamed.

Sinking into his chair, he wondered about Abby. What was she doing? Did she love sunny Florida? Had she already started her new job?

Did she miss him as much as he missed her?

He dropped his head into his hands and squeezed his temples to ease the dull ache. Sending her away had been the right thing to do, but he couldn't stand the thought that she might hate him for it. Although she hadn't hated him for the part he'd unwittingly played in Shane's death. Maybe she could forgive him for this, too?

What if she wasn't happy? He lifted his head to stare out the window. He knew a big part of her leaving had to do with escaping her family. Maybe she was miserable without them.

Or maybe this was all wishful thinking on his part.

Nick started in on the stack of policies needing review. He'd made his choice and she'd made hers. He needed to remember that.

"What happened to Dr Roland, your first medical director?" Two weeks later, Abby found herself seated across from Charlotte, her new boss at Lee County Hospital. The woman from the traveling nurse company had sent all her information to Charlotte, who spent a long hour reviewing the information. "I see, by this letter, he was recently replaced by a Dr Tremayne?"

"Yes." Abby fidgeted in her seat. She didn't want to go into great detail, but worried the woman would disregard Nick's letter if she didn't explain. "Dr Roland had some personal problems, which interfered with his medical care of our patients, so I had no choice but to report him to Hospital Administration and the AMA. As a result, our chief of staff asked for his resignation."

"Really?" Charlotte's eyes rounded. "I'm sure it wasn't easy for you to report him to the American Medical Association. Wow. You've had quite an interesting career."

Seeing her life through the eyes of a stranger made Abby sit up straighter in her chair. She'd never considered everything that had gone on with Dr Roland as interesting or exciting. Yet there was no mistaking the awed expression in Charlotte's eyes. The woman probably wouldn't look so impressed if she'd heard how Roland had slapped her. Abby resisted the urge to cover her cheek.

After a few minutes of chit-chat, Charlotte seemed satisfied so Abby picked up her schedule and left. But Charlotte's words followed her on the long walk home. Had she been so intent on seeking excitement that she hadn't recognized the experience when it had smacked her in the face? Nagging doubt assailed her and her footsteps slowed.

Could Nick be right? Was she so busy trying to escape from her overprotective family that she used traveling as an excuse to avoid dealing with them? Had she really let Alec annoy her so much she'd moved a thousand miles from home?

And left Nick?

A loud crash from the open door of a restaurant diverted her attention from her thoughts. "Help! This man needs help!"

After a moment of hesitation, Abby scurried inside. She blinked, forcing her eyes to adjust to the dimly lit room. "What is it? What's wrong?"

"I think he's having a heart attack!" A skinny guy wearing a chocolate-smeared apron and with a long gray ponytail hanging down his back wrung his hands in dismay.

Abby dropped to her knees beside a large, chalky-faced man who looked far too young to be suffering from a heart attack. He sat on the floor in a daze, surrounded by remnants of broken plates and saucers.

"What's wrong?" She checked his pulse, not surprised to find a rapid pace. His skin was clammy and diaphoretic. Cripes, regardless of how young he was, she suspected he really was having a myocardial infarction.

"Feels like…I can't get…my breath."

"Call 911 and get me a baby aspirin." Too bad she didn't have any nitroglycerin tablets with her. Or an oxygen tank. Or a darned stethoscope. The skinny man in the apron rushed to the phone.

"I want you to sit here and try to relax." Not an easy task, she was certain. She tried to calm her own racing heart. "I'm a nurse. You'll find it easier to get your breath if you just close your eyes for a minute and try to relax." She hoped her smile was reassuring. "What's your name?"

"Dorian."

"My name is Abby. I'm going to stay right here with you until the ambulance arrives."

Dorian's hopeful expression crumpled. "Ambulance? Am I that sick?"

"I don't have any baby aspirin." The guy with the ponytail whined, returning from the depths of the kitchen. "Just regular aspirin."

"That will work fine. We'll cut it in half." If the ponytail guy fell apart, she'd have two basket cases on her hands. Not good. "I need you to fetch him some water."

She managed to maintain control until the screeching of sirens filled the air. As the noise grew louder, Dorian's heart rate shot up dramatically.

"Relax, Dorian, slow your breathing. The faster you breathe, the more oxygen your body needs. And that means less oxygen is available for your heart." She couldn't lose him now when help was so near. "Look at me, I'm right here. I won't leave you. You're going to be fine."

She repeated her mantra while the sirens halted outside the open door. Laden with equipment, the paramedics rushed in.

Thankful for the additional help, she held on to Dorian's hand and explained what had happened. "His pulse is tachy at 126 and his respirations are 30 and shallow. He's been extremely diaphoretic and I've given him half an aspirin."

"Good work." The paramedic closest to her was about her age and extremely handsome with his beach-blond looks and dark tan. He flashed her a very interested smile as he looped oxygen tubing over Dorian's ears and inserted the prongs in his nose. "Why don't you tag along with us during the rest of our shift? We could use the help."

She gave him a tense smile. "No, thanks, I start my new job at Lee County hospital tomorrow as it is." She took the leads from the other paramedic and placed them on Dorian's chest. "These are so we can see what's going on with your heart," she explained.

"OK." Dorian clutched her hand as soon as she'd finished.

The beach-blond paramedic deftly started an IV in Dorian's arm. Once he had the fluid running, he pretended to sigh. "Lee County, huh? Tell me your name, I'll look you up. We make runs there fairly often."

She held her tongue, her brief moment of humor fading into annoyance with the guy's persistence in flirting with her when they had a patient to take care of. She held the patient's gaze. "Dorian, listen, can you hear your heartbeat on the monitor?"

He nodded, his eyes wide.

"You're doing just fine," Abby reassured him.

Moments later, they had Dorian safely tucked onto the gurney. She hung onto Dorian's hand until the point where they slid him into the back of the ambulance. The beach-blond paramedic shot her one last sexy smile before closing the doors behind him.

"Is he going to be all right?" the gray-haired, apron-wearing man asked from behind her.

"I'm sure he'll be fine. You can call the hospital in a little while to check on him." Abby glanced at the mess on the floor. "Do you need help?"

"Nah, unless you're willing to wash dishes?" His expression turned hopeful.

"I don't think so. I have to get going." Abby beat a quick retreat.

After leaving the restaurant, she continued toward her condo. But the delay with Dorian had given the dark stormclouds a head start. There was streak of lightning, followed by a deep warning rumble of thunder.

Her spirits sank. *Don't rain, don't rain.* Abby picked up her pace, jogging despite the sandals on her feet. She wanted to turn back. Washing dishes didn't seem nearly as bad as walking through a pouring rainstorm.

The deluge of rain hit when she was still several blocks from her condo. Swearing beneath her breath, she ran, ignoring her pinched toes in the uncomfortably wet sandals. The water came down so hard she could barely see, especially with her hair dripping in her eyes.

When she dashed up the stairs to her second-floor condo, she saw the dark looming shape a moment too late. She plowed against a distinctly male form.

Not the blond paramedic? For a moment panic flared, until a familiar pair of strong hands wrapped around her arms.

"Abby? Are you all right?"

"Nick?" She shoved a fistful of wet hair from her eyes. Could she have looked any less attractive? "What are you doing here?"

"Waiting for you." He pulled her toward her doorway. "Let's get inside. You need to dry off so you won't get sick."

A strangled laugh caught in her throat. "I've been caught in the rain so much, I wouldn't know what dry is." Still, she dug in her pocket for her key then gave it to him.

Inside, she ducked into her bedroom and hastily stripped out of her wet clothes and toweled herself dry. Why had Nick come? Did he have news from home?

Bad news?

Throwing on a robe, she shot back into the living area. "Is something wrong? My parents? Alec? Beth?"

Nick held up a hand. "Nothing is wrong. Your family is fine, Abby. They send their love."

"Thank God." Abby let out a deep breath. "For a moment I thought…well, never mind." Feeling awkward, she tightened the belt on her robe. "I'm surprised to see you."

Nick looked wonderful. Not as handsome as the beach-blond paramedic, but her pulse skipped a beat when he held her gaze. "I needed to see you. I miss you, Abby."

"Oh, Nick." Her façade of indifference crumbled and she threw herself into his arms. "I miss you, too."

"Abby, I know how much you want to travel." Nick spoke in a low voice near her ear as he held her close. "But I can't stop thinking of you."

"I've found traveling isn't very much fun when you're all alone." Her words were muffled against his chest.

There was a long pause, then Nick gently pulled away. "Hey, I didn't mean to get all maudlin here. How's your new job? I have a lot to tell you. I've started the planning for relocating the physical therapy gym to the second floor. Will you come and see it on your next visit back?"

Abby stared at him, the abrupt change of subject catching her off guard, then understood. He thought she was asking him to leave his job and travel with her. Her stomach sank like a rock. "Of course I will, but first I have to explain something to you. Remember what you said about me leaving for the right reasons?"

He nodded, his gaze questioning.

"You were right. I was running from my family. I love them dearly, but they were making me so nuts. Especially Alec, who sees drug dealers on every corner." She tunneled her fingers through her wet hair. "But you know what? I've figured out while I've been here that I can be independent and remain close to home. I stood up to Roland, didn't I?"

"Are you saying what I think you're saying?" Nick asked.

She laughed. "I think so. I've committed to three months, so I have to stay at least that long, but then I can leave. I can return home. I love my family and I know they love me. I was so stupid to use traveling as an excuse to run."

"Not stupid, Abby." His smile was crooked. "I know what it's like to want to see the world. You deserve that chance."

"Some day." Abby shrugged. She couldn't really find any reason to care. Seeing the world paled compared to spending time with Nick. "And we can always rack up a pile of frequent flyer miles during the next few months."

Nick's smile faded. "Abby, I know you're young and have your whole future ahead of you, but…will you marry me?"

"Yes, I'll marry you. I love you. Even if you are pig-headed. We *both* have our whole lives ahead of us, not just me. When are you going to figure that out?"

"When I have a wedding ring safely secured on your

finger." Nick leaned over to pull her back into his arms. "You won't regret this, Abby. I promise. I love you. More than you'll ever know."

Her heart soared at his words. "I love you, too."

"I'll take you anyplace in the whole world for our honeymoon," he continued earnestly. "You name the spot."

"Hmm." She pretended to think. "Italy has always been one place I've longed to see." She leaned up to wrap her arms around his neck and pulled him down for a kiss as giddy happiness swelled in her heart. When she eventually broke off the kiss, because she needed to breathe, she added, "But it doesn't matter where we go, Nick. As long as afterward we return home."

FREE!
4 Books
and a surprise gift!

We would like to take this opportunity to thank you for reading this Mills & Boon® book by offering you the chance to take FOUR more specially selected titles from the Medical Romance™ series absolutely FREE! We're also making this offer to introduce you to the benefits of the Reader Service™—

- ★ FREE home delivery
- ★ FREE gifts and competitions
- ★ FREE monthly Newsletter
- ★ Exclusive Reader Service offers
- ★ Books available before they're in the shops

Accepting these FREE books and gift places you under no obligation to buy, you may cancel at any time, even after receiving your free shipment. Simply complete your details below and return the entire page to the address below. You don't even need a stamp!

YES! Please send me 4 free Medical Romance books and a surprise gift. I understand that unless you hear from me, I will receive 6 superb new titles every month for just £2.80 each, postage and packing free. I am under no obligation to purchase any books and may cancel my subscription at any time. The free books and gift will be mine to keep in any case.

M6ZEF

Ms/Mrs/Miss/Mr .... Initials ....

BLOCK CAPITALS PLEASE

Surname ....

Address ....

....

.... Postcode ....

Send this whole page to:
UK: FREEPOST CN81, Croydon, CR9 3WZ